1

<u>Brigade</u>

a novel

TR Pearson

Barking Mad Press

Whit

1

We don't get a lot of company in the small hours of the morning. My house is probably a quarter mile off the road, and Bootsy would have barked if a car had come up since she only ever barks at cars. Instead, she was upside down and crowding me hard when the pounding started.

I lurched over to the closet to fetch my rifle, an ancient Savage over and under, and I carried it into the living room and shouted toward the front door, "What?"

The pounding got more frantic. There was a bit of yelling as well, a string of words I couldn't quite make out.

I suspected somebody had run off the road and ended up in my soybean patch since I'd seen that sort of thing a good half dozen times already. The blacktop bends in front of my place, and nobody these days only drives. I unbolted my door and opened it as far as the night chain would allow.

A hand pushed in through the crack. The knuckles were bloody. There was rope around the wrist. I threw the switch, and the porch light revealed a filthy, wretched woman in a foul t-shirt and panties. I couldn't understand what she was saying, but I know pleading when I hear it, so I dropped the chain, drew the door full open, and waved her on inside.

She smelled like she'd been living in a bear den, had that sour, feral stink you sometimes nose up in the woods. It was enough to bring Bootsy off the bed. She circled and sniffed and growled. Bootsy looks a bit like a groundhog, is squat and inordinately homely, and she's less a pet and companion than a fur-bearing ordeal.

"What happened to you?" I asked that woman and got back a bunch of foreign chatter.

Her t-shirt had been sky-blue once, and there was a chimp's face printed on it. He was wearing a bellboy's cap and had the words Cheez Monkey!! above his head. That shirt was ripped and stained, not even rag-worthy, and it barely reached the top of her panties. They were filthy, girly cotton things with black-eyed Susans in the weave.

"I'm going to call the cops," I told her. I added, "Police." I said it slow and loud like you do with people who insist on being foreign.

The girl seemed fine about it until I'd fetched my phone off the sideboard when she shook her head and grabbed at me, said emphatic stuff my way.

"PO-lice." I tried it louder and slower.

She rattled off something rapid-fire and snatched the phone out of my hand. I was just a half-awake dirt farmer in a pair of pajama bottoms, so I can't say I had much grip on what I ought to do. She talked at me as she went down my hallway. Bootsy followed her, growling. The girl turned on the bathroom light.

"You want to wash up? Is that it?"

She said something back and stepped into the bathroom, still carrying my phone. She shut the door behind her, and I soon heard the shower running.

I fetched a shirt for me and a robe for her. Once the shower was off, I tapped on the bathroom door, and she opened it buck naked. She was cleaner but scabby and welted up, bruised and dinged all over. I handed her the robe, and she gave me her nasty panties and her filthy t-shirt, which I tossed onto the back porch to let them stink outside.

She ate everything I put in front of her, including a pint of freezer-burned sherbet.

I smacked my chest and told her, "Whit." She said back, "Besa," while she chewed. Then she slipped out of her dinette chair and straight under the table where she curled up on the linoleum and went to sleep.

Bootsy joined her, and I grabbed the quilt off the sofa and threw it over the pair of them, decided to let it all keep until morning and went to bed myself.

She didn't wake up when I brewed the coffee or when I dragged Bootsy out from under the quilt to make her go outside. She even kept on sleeping when Salvador let himself in and gave me an "Ola." He saw the girl soon thereafter and pointed inquiringly her way.

"Came knocking."

Salvador eased in for a better look. "Where from?"

I shrugged.

"She not saying?"

"Not in English. Had this on her." I showed him the loop of rope I'd picked up off the bathroom floor.

Right then she twitched and started awake, sat up and banged her head on a chair seat. She came out with a burst of chatter, racket an indignant chicken might make.

Salvador told her, "Ola," as well.

I more or less inherited Salvador from a shiftless second cousin, a boy named Dudley who'd gone into the Christmas tree business, which was more of a tax dodge for him than anything else. He'd run across Salvador at a lumber yard and had hired him on part-time. Salvador was working mostly odd jobs back then and didn't yet have his proper papers, so he wasn't awfully picky about who he took work from.

They planted thirty acres of Nordmann firs in a spot where you'd be lucky to get a slash pine to grow. Of course, the idea was to take a loss and write off inflated expenses, but Dudley never got around to bringing Salvador up to speed on that. Dudley had gone in counting on Mexicans being a touch more worthless than he was, but Salvador proved to be industrious and more than a little inventive, and he figured out how to amend the soil to make those fir trees thrive.

That tore it for Dudley. He knew the boy helping me had gone off to Parris Island, so he drove Salvador over, pulled up in my yard, and said essentially, "Here."

Salvador had a wife in Mexico and two American girlfriends. Not always the same two. He'd swap them out as he went along, needed them chiefly for the dancing he got up to on most weekends, some kind of fancy two-step from down in Zacatecas.

Salvador coaxed Besa onto a chair. "Where you coming from, honey?" he asked her.

She told him back plenty, all of it in her mother tongue.

"What's she talking?"

Salvador shook his head. *"Buenos Dias,"* he said. *"Bonjour. God Morgan. Namaste. Huomenta."*

Salvador was a regular magpie where it came to languages of the world. He spoke English and Spanish and some kind of Creole, enough Italian to regularly make the waitress at our local spagoo joint howl.

*"Raam raam. Bon dia. Dobroe utro."*

That last one seemed to hit her half right. She said something like, *"Buna dimineata"* back.

"Mine's Russian," Salvador told me. "Not too sure what hers is."

We both watched her sip coffee.

"Skinny thing," he said. "Let's make her some eggs."

I went over to the stove and pulled my skillet out of the drawer.

"That boy with the body shop out past Flint Top. He's Russian or something, isn't he?"

"Helsinki," Salvador told me. "Where are the cops in all of this?"

"She wouldn't let me call them."

Salvador rose from the table and came over with his mug. "Could be one of those mail-order things gone bad?"

I nodded. I was at that stage in life where I wouldn't put any damn thing past any damn body.

Besa finished her eggs, ate them with her fingers, and then licked her plate. She slipped down onto the linoleum where she curled up like a cat and went to sleep.

Me and Salvador had planned on a day of swapping out fence posts in my cow lot, so that's what we went ahead and did while Besa napped. I couldn't get past the bother involved in keeping a girl tied up, and since most of my neighbors were variations on my worthless cousin, hostage taking hardly seemed a likely local enterprise.

"Most of these boys can't even keep livestock," I told Salvador.

"Probably started out simple, got worse," he said. "What trash you got in walking distance?"

I did a mental inventory and picked out a candidate or two. "Luther maybe?"

"With the pigs?"

I nodded. "Or that Snyder boy. The middle one."

"Isn't that little fat thing his wife? You know, with the mouth?"

"Might have wanted one he couldn't understand."

We were pulling fence posts and replacing them all along, so this wasn't our best considered and well-reasoned conversation. I just tossed out names as they came to me, and Salvador shot them down.

We'd settled on a kind of plan by the time we got back into the kitchen. Besa and Bootsy were under the table, both of them dead asleep. Salvador fished out the pimento cheese while I found my county map, and once the girl was awake and fed some more, I spread that map out on the table.

"Us," I told her and pointed at the floor and then tapped the map in the appropriate spot.

Besa eyed the map. Eyed me and Salvador. She told us a string of something. I tapped the map another time and pointed at the floor again.

She did us the favor of studying the thing in a vague and general sort of way. I couldn't really blame her since it was mostly green crosshatching with numbered county roads and the odd stream working through.

"I don't think she's getting it," I said to Salvador.

So he tapped and pointed and told her, "Us," more loudly than I had.

She said something further as she plucked a ballpoint out of my pen and pencil mug and started drawing something on a napkin.

"A cat?" Salvador asked me.

"Uh uh," I told him. "Believe it's a cow."

She'd drawn a particular sort of cow, and I happened to recognize it. She'd made the creature black on either end and had left it napkin-white in the middle.

"And I think I know just where she means," I said and country pointed toward the backside of the house. "I used to buy hay from a boy out through there, would drive right by that place. They kept Belted Galloways. Had a sign up for them."

We went over in Salvador's Cherokee, a beast of thing with assorted saints epoxied to the front dash and Jesus in a sunset where the headliner used to be. I fished Salvador's .22 out of the glovebox and dropped the clip for a look — only four bullets. Besa was still wearing my bathrobe and sat in the back with Bootsy on her lap.

"Don't think anybody lives there now," I told Salvador. "Sign's knocked over. Just caught my eye, you know?"

I directed him off the blacktop and down a dirt road to a track, which got so little traffic it had grass growing up the middle.

Salvador eased over where I told him, and we all got out and walked to the spot where a honeysuckle thicket ended at a rusty cattle grate. I pointed out the painted sign half laying in the shrubbery. It featured a soulful rendition, about two feet square, of a heifer in profile. Black on either end with a white strip in the middle.

Besa sure got chatty when she saw it, more than a little agitated, and she went over the grate and waved for us to follow her up the drive.

The farmhouse on the crown of the rise was a federalist four on four that hadn't seen paint since Roosevelt was a boy. The clapboards looked bleached and etched by the weather, and the porch roof had partly collapsed. The window holes were mostly vacant, no glass or sashes either one.

"Let me," I said to Salvador and Besa both since I was the one with the gun.

The front door wasn't entirely shut. I crossed the porch and shouldered it open. There wasn't much to see but grit and trash, a sooty stove pipe, a funeral home calendar hanging on the back wall. That house stank of vermin and mildew, and all the rooms I wandered through were in a similar state. I didn't bother to go upstairs since four or five of the treads were missing.

I just shouted, "Hey!" a couple of times but didn't get anything back.

Salvador and Besa were where I left them.

"Ask her where she was tied up."

Salvador asked Besa every version of donde? he could manage.

She gave him back a freshet of chatter and then set off around the house. Besa led us to a pair of rusty bulkhead cellar doors. They were locked together at the hasp, but the top hinge of one had busted, and that door had been shifted around to make a gap a girl could probably fit through.

Salvador fired up his phone light and stuck his head in for a look. He pulled back out pretty quick.

"Thunder bucket. Rope and mess." He glanced at the house, the collapsed barn across the way, the overgrown pasture with most of the fencing laid over. "Who owns this place?"

"Don't know. No cows on it for a while."

Besa seemed remarkably composed for a woman brought back to the hole she'd been stowed in.

"Some damn body needs arresting," Salvador said.

I was feeling the same way and nodded. That's about when we heard it off across the pasture, the high-pitched mosquito whine of a motorbike coming our way.

The sound of it appeared to rattle Besa. She said a couple of frantic things and slipped behind a big, scraggly hollyhock bush at the corner of the house. She kept talking and waving at us until we'd joined her there.

That motorbike closed hard, and then the engine died. A kid came around the far corner, a boy with scraggly hair. He looked fourteen or fifteen, but who can tell anymore, and he was carrying a blue pail, one of those plastic beach buckets that children use for messing around in the sand.

We watched him see the busted hinge. It stopped him and confused him. You could almost smell the brain oil as he tried to settle on what to do. Then he saw us or sniffed us out or something, eyed our bush anyway and dropped his bucket and bolted.

Me and Salvador chased him but only got so far as that sand pail. It had tipped over and spilled its contents. Brown lettuce, a greasy pork chop bone, a chunk of bread heel, and what looked like potato salad. There was a cigarette butt and a balled up napkin as well.

The motorbike engine fired up, and that boy raced back the way he'd come while me and Salvador stood there considering the slop.

Besa, for her part, came straight over and gave that pail a kick.

We all looked up as that boy throttled down. He'd stopped in the middle of the pasture. He turned our way and fiddled with something, and we finally heard the racket from his gun. The bullet went high and hit a clapboard ten feet up.

Salvador suggested, "Shoot him back."

At that distance, a bullet from Salvador's pistol might have left only a bruise, so I was happy enough to take dead aim and fire four times in rapid succession. I hit the motorbike at least once because we all heard the bullet ping.

That boy throttled up and took off, and his motorbike went sputtering and whining across the pasture until he dipped down a slope when we couldn't see him or hear him anymore.

We carried Besa directly to the shopping plaza and into the Peebles in my housecoat where we had her pick out some actual clothes, and she went with a cotton dress. It was kind of a smock with wheat sheaves on it, and we bought her some underthings and flip-flops, a brush and hair clip too. Besa fixed herself up in the back of the Cherokee while Salvador drove to the county PD, and she was fine until he eased into the lot where all the cruisers parked.

The girl pitched such an extravagant fit, protested with such volume and vigor as to prompt Salvador to pull straight back into the road.

"Got an idea," I told Salvador and directed him to the bypass out toward Brisco where all the auto lots and dollar stores are anymore.

Former state trooper Avery McCloud worked at the Chevrolet place, and I went in and found him at the service counter. He'd pulled me once on the interstate for disconnected trailer lights but had just called me a knucklehead and let me go. He'd retired from the force a couple of years back and (by the looks of him) started living on bundt cake.

"Whit. Hell, buddy."

"Got a minute for me?" I motioned toward the door I'd just come in, and he followed me out.

"Car trouble?" He was looking at Salvador's Cherokee by then.

"Not exactly."

I started in on a version of Besa's story but kept having to pause for enlargements whenever Avery said, "Hold on. What?"

Salvador and Besa left the Jeep as we closed. I made the introductions.

"Who scuffed her up?"

"Not sure yet. It's like this," and I acquainted Avery with Besa's objection to the law.

"Well . . ." Avery smiled as he gave Besa his full consideration. "I know a boy who might could sniff around some, see what you got hold of. You willing to go out of pocket?"

"I guess," I said. "A little. He some kind of cop?"

"Used to be. Brings his truck in sometimes."

The guy Avery knew lived down in the river bottom where they grow rice anymore. He didn't grow any himself, just sticker bushes and Johnson grass, and he had a feedlot with a donkey in it, but that proved to be happenstance. The gate was gone, and the donkey came wandering over once we'd pulled up.

There was a Chevy king cab in the yard along with a Grand Prix carcass, an old rusty glider upended on a pile of pallets and compound buckets. A disassembled lawn tractor took up most of the front porch.

That donkey zeroed in on Salvador and shoved him with her snout. He shoved her back. Salvador had a colorful personal history with donkeys, and like a donkey will, she proved determined to plague the guy who'd like it least.

I didn't have to knock. He was standing on the other side of the door screen eating a chicken leg.

"Mr. Tatum? Delray Tatum?"

"Ray," he said.

I explained about Avery.

"Yeah. He called."

"Think you can help us?" I asked him.

Ray looked the three of us over in a leisurely way. He had another bite of chicken. "Doubt it," he finally said.

2

Ray's house on the inside was spare and neat. Beyond tidy. Antiseptic. He had a sofa and a couple of ladder-back chairs, a stack of library books on the floor. A tiger oak sideboard. No TV. Ray offered us coffee but didn't mean it.

Me and Salvador went through the entire Besa episode for Ray who heard us out and asked in time, "Toward Purvis?"

That was about where the Galloway farm had been. I nodded. "Road just past the Dollar General. Doesn't go all the way through."

Ray stepped over to his sideboard and tugged open a drawer, pulled out a gazetteer for the entire state.

"Show me."

I did.

"Where'd the boy go?"

Between us, me and Salvador traced a route across pastureland that ended at a dead-end county road on the far side of a stream.

"Doctor seen her?"

I hadn't thought of that and shook my head.

"Think she'll stand for it?" Ray asked us and winked at Besa who told him a string of stuff.

We shrugged.  Who could say what Besa would stand for?

Ray fished his phone out of his pocket and went scrolling through his numbers, which I took as an opportunity to visit the head.

I slipped down a brief hallway, eased past the bathroom, and had a nosy peek into the bedrooms on either side.  Both tidy. No strewn clothes. Shoes all lined up.  The bed I took for Ray's was neatly made while the one across the hall was stripped down to the mattress. There was a rolling rack next to it, the kind you hang IV bags from. The artwork over the bed was a jagged paint-by-numbers alpine scene.

"Doc'll see us at five," Salvador told me once I'd stepped back into the front room.

"Happy to pay you something," I said to Ray, "if you're willing to nose around."

"You boys don't even know what you're looking at yet. If it's rape, that's for the cops. Hayseed bullshit? Who the hell knows? I might can help with that."

That seemed sensible. I told him, "All right."

"Doesn't even have to be money." Ray glanced at Salvador as he spoke. "Kind of like that donkey off my hands."

Salvador made the brand of noise you make when the thing you hate most is a donkey and a man is threatening to give you one instead of taking pay.

"Where you going to keep her?" I asked him once we were on the main road proper.

"Carport freezer maybe. Bottom of my pond."

Ray's doctor friend worked out of a clinic two towns over, just east of the highway and hard by a Hunan Buffet. We killed an hour in the parking lot, didn't try to explain it to Besa. Instead, I bought her an order of ribs to work on while we waited.

The reception girl finally came out to fetch us. They were slipping us in just after hours, and we all got crowded into an exam room about the size of a sedan. There was a poster on the wall that featured photos of various diseased organs — the sort of stuff you usually see in a veterinarian's office along with a wormy heart in a jar.

The doctor came in still talking to somebody in the hallway. She had a boy's regular haircut and the manner of a prison guard. She glanced at me and Salvador, paid most of her heed to Besa.

"Ray said you'd . . ." but before I could finish, she told us, "Gentlemen," and jabbed a thumb toward the door.

I flipped through a year-old Us! magazine out in the waiting room while Salvador listed (as they occurred to him) the reasons why I was the one who needed a donkey instead of him.

Soon enough the doctor showed up and motioned to us. We followed her back down the corridor and into that puny exam room. Besa was wearing a backless paper smock and standing in a corner, and she opened up on us but good the moment we came in.

"Who are you to her?" the doctor asked us.

I gave her the abbreviated version.

"She all right?" Salvador wanted to know.

"She look all right?"

We were used to the state of Besa by then. "Kind of rough," I allowed to the doctor.

"She's been knocked around pretty good. No vaginal tearing that I could see. Ray's on this at least. That's something," she said. "He won't quit, and he probably needs a distraction."

I remembered that IV rack in his spare room. "Somebody die?"

The doc handed Besa her Peebles dress. "Ask him."

We stopped at the Food Lion on the way home, and I bought some decent, healthy stuff and a hell of a lot more crackers. Since Salvador had a girlfriend to squire, he left us straightaway, and I parked Besa in front of the Weather Channel while I cooked her up a stir fry I served to her on the sofa. She left all the broccoli and the crinkle cut carrots, just picked the chicken and garlic out. Then she and Bootsy crawled under the dinette table and went to sleep.

I phoned Ray and gave him the doctor's report. It was a little like talking to an open line. He listened. He breathed. I finished and waited.

"Can y'all go around with me tomorrow?" he finally asked.

"Probably so."

Ray grunted. That proved to be his sign off, which I realized only after a while.

He showed up at half-past seven in the morning, beat Salvador by a quarter hour, and me and him stood out at my pasture fence with an audience of cows. Half Herefords and half Charolais because that's what I could get. They slapped their tails and chomped and snorted, evacuated freely.

One of my bulls came over for an up close, almost forensic look at Ray. I could understand the attraction since Ray had a glacial quality about him. Ray just stayed where he was and eyed that big boy back.

Ray had brought his gazetteer and rode up front with Salvador who identified for Ray the various saints epoxied to his Cherokee dashboard.

"St. Kateri," he said and pointed. "That's Mohawk for Catherine. This one here's St. Peregrine. Cured himself of foot cancer. See how his leg sticks out?"

Ray endured him as he consulted his gazetteer. He gave Salvador the occasional direction while Besa said foreign stuff to me in the back. We traded a proper paved and painted road for a janky, patched blacktop that went eventually to oiled hardpan and then sparse gravel with runs of mud.

We'd ride for stretches with just woods on either side and then come to a shingled farmhouse or a trailer, usually with bright, plastic kid stuff and an incinerator barrel in the yard. We didn't see many people, just some geezer on the roadside who looked like he'd passed an hour or two rolling around in the ditch.

"Got to be back in here somewhere," Ray finally said as we entered a chunk of landscape that didn't appear to be much of anywhere at all. Scrub pines and car tires and a couple of tumbledown chimneys. It took Ray's eye to spy the track that snaked back into the woods.

"Hold on."

Salvador stopped, and Ray climbed out and stepped into a break in the scrub where the ground was pine needles and black mucky dirt. When the rest of us joined him, he pointed out a tread print. Single tire. Single track that ran into a thicket.

"Why don't y'all hang back," he told us.

We didn't hang back, of course. We bunched up right behind him and followed Ray through the woods, which in truth was more of a farm field long neglected and overgrown. There were slash pines and saplings and leggy ironwood trees, a world of human trash — antifreeze jugs, and soda bottles, and enough Milwaukee's Best cans to nearly qualify as mulch.

I'd say we walked a good quarter mile before we came to a run of jackleg fencing, a couple of strands of barbed wire tacked to anything that would do with a stretch of it laying over on the ground.

We spied more human mess up ahead. A shed or something and the usual warty heaps of garbage. Ray pointed out a motorbike leaning against a poplar.

"That it?"

"Maybe. Probably. I think I shot it."

He eased up for a closer look and put his finger on a .22 caliber sized divot in the frame. There was a goat in the yard and a couple of roosters, or in the weedy clearing anyway that appeared to pass for a yard. The house beyond the shed was an asbestos-shingled box with a couple of topside dormer windows and a back door standing half open.

We hung where we were and watched Ray mount the back steps. He knocked to no answer and then gently ease inside.

He came back out shortly. "Know him?" Ray asked Besa as he showed her his phone screen.

Salvador tried to weigh in with the Russian version, but it wasn't really needed since we got the drift from Besa who spat with some high feeling onto the ground.

When I finally got a decent look at Ray's phone myself, I could see the guy was done for from his open, milky eye.

Ray pointed at the back door by way of telling me and Salvador to step on in and have a look if we wanted. Salvador wasn't game, but I was and stuck my head into the house. There were flies and a bit of a stink, though nothing overpowering, just the mineral smell of spilled blood and rot and decay setting in. The dead guy was on the kitchen floor, mostly on the floor anyway but half leaning against a cabinet under the sink. His blood had all left him through holes in his neck, a matching set, one on either side.

It was hardly like he was spoiling the decor. The place was a landfill under rafters with crap and squalor just about everywhere crap and squalor could be.

Ray soon joined me.

"Clean work," I said of the wounds.

He nodded.

"You check around for the boy?"

He shook his head. I followed him through the house. We visited all the downstairs rooms and then headed up the staircase. There was clutter and junk but no people anywhere. Greasy bedsheets. Clothes piled on the floor.

Over by one of the dormer windows, Ray got enough of a signal to call out. I saw him punch in 9-1-1.

We did an awful lot of talking to county officials out in that buggy yard, all of us but Besa who got real quiet and mostly watched the ground. We'd tell a chunk of our story to one cop, and then he'd bring in a buddy and have us tell the same thing all over again. The forensic people kept moving in and out of the house, guys in paper suits and booties who looked about half keen on their jobs.

They did quite a lot of milling around and smoking until the sheriff showed up. He didn't wear a uniform and had us call him Rowdy, looked like he hadn't quite accepted how far from Texas he was. He had on jeans and boots and one of those cowboy shirts with snaps on the pockets. His belt buckle was the size of a salad plate. His hat was a mouse-gray Open Road.

"Look here, would you," the sheriff said. "If it isn't Delray Tatum."

Ray lifted his chin ever so slightly by way of hello.

"Haven't hardly seen you since Meekins and them."

That seemed right to Ray. He nodded.

"And what's this thing with the girl?" The sheriff looked my way. "You say she knocked on your door?"

I told him all the stuff I'd told the rest of them already.

One of the techs in a jumpsuit handed the sheriff what looked like a driver's license in a baggie. Rowdy squinted at the thing, tried to make his arms longer.

"Maxwell Hector Delaney. Know him?"

We didn't and said so.

"Mostly Kinnocks back in here, isn't it?" The sheriff was talking to a brawny deputy who nodded. Then Rowdy turned our way. "Y'all need to come on to the station so we can see what's what." Then he went swaggering over to the back door and straight into the house.

We all watched him. That seemed kind of what he was after.

"The man's from Steubenville," Ray told us. "Couldn't saddle a horse with a gun to his head."

Me and Ray and Besa got put in the back of a cruiser. They let Salvador fetch his Cherokee and drive himself to the station house. On the way, I talked to Ray a little since there was no real talking to Besa.

"You know him?"

Ray nodded. "Worked with him once."

"Meekins and them?"

"Murder-suicide that wasn't." Ray paused a quarter minute. "Murder-murder," he said.

Then he went back to watching scenery while Besa told me a thing or three and gave the evil eye to the musclehead behind the wheel.

Sheriff Rowdy had gotten out from under his Stetson by the time we saw him again, and he was one of those guys who looked like somebody else without his hat. He doled us out to rooms where we could sit and answer questions. I got a lady deputy with a schizophrenic streak.

She was part gentle Christian, part bad cop and took turns appealing to my sense of decency and threatening me with consequences. Her name was Gwen, and by God you called her that or nothing.

"So you were asleep?"

"Yes, ma'am."

"Gwen. And she came knocking?"

"Right. Around two, I think."

"And you just let her in?"

"Had a look at her, but yes, ma'am."

"Gwen. You in the habit of opening your door to strangers in the middle of the night?"

"No, ma'am, not really."

"Gwen."

Deputy Gwen smelled like Jolly Ranchers and Merit Lights. She was wearing two different earrings, had a stud hole in her nose, and I felt sure she was inked on her calves and shoulders. Gwen was that kind of girl.

I went through all of it three or four times over. I could hear Besa in the room next door saying something foreign loudly.

"Get her translated," I suggested. "You guys'll figure this out quick." Then I stood up and stretched. "That'll do for now."

I left the room before Gwen could settle on what she needed to say to stop me.

I found Salvador sitting in the hallway getting an earful from Sheriff Rowdy. I heard enough to know straightaway it was a Mexican thing. Something about papers and rights and privileges.

"Where you going?" the sheriff asked me.

"To let my dog out. He's got to take me." I pointed Salvador's way. "Ray still here?"

"In with your girl."

"Tell him we'll be back in a while."

"We're not done with you boys by a hell of a stretch."

"We know." I said to Salvador, "Come on."

Bootsy was unhappy. I can't quite say why since she'd held nothing back and had done all her business on my kitchen floor. Not on the tile, of course, but on the throw rug in front of the sink, which I'd shampooed all I was meaning to and so chucked it into the yard.

Salvador made us sandwiches, and we ate them sitting on my porch steps.

"What do you figure?" he asked me.

"Probably started as Satan's lapdog and got out of hell somehow."

"I mean Besa and her stuff."

I shrugged and chewed and grunted.

"I bet they know all about her by now," he told me.

I had my doubts. I'd been a deputy for a little while, so I'd seen it all up close — county cops banging keyboards with their doughy index fingers. They could usually roll prints and take mugshots well enough, but things often got scattered and dicey after that.

"You don't need to go back," I told Salvador. "I can lay it all out for them." I was thinking of Sheriff Rowdy and that wetback rubbish he'd been talking.

Salvador polished off his sandwich and shook his head. "I don't steer wide of asshats."

So it was both of us who found Besa sitting in the hallway shackled to a bench, and Deputy Gwen came along to explain, "She crawled through the window in the ladies', ended up in the road."

Salvador tried some of his scant Russian on Besa, and she gave him an agitated earful back.

"What all's she saying?" Deputy Gwen wanted to know.

"You know," Salvador told her. "Hey and stuff."

They'd cast around for a translator and had found a teacher at the college in the valley who the sheriff had prevailed upon to drive over after her last class. She wasn't happy about it. We saw her come in — me and Salvador and Besa. The word she used on Gwen and Rowdy was 'dragooned'.

It turned out she taught French primarily, and she'd make spirited, Gallic asides like *allons-y!* or *droit du seigneur*, and sometimes just *merde!* She ended up talking to Besa on the bench out in the hall because Besa raised a violent fuss whenever they tried to move her. So the professor sat and quizzed her in every language she could dredge up, which was French and Italian, a smattering of German, and a bit of menu Greek.

"What's she speaking?" Sheriff Rowdy wanted to know and got a tutorial on glottal stops and fricatives, which struck me as a pretty transparent variety of academic stalling. Since the woman couldn't say exactly what language Besa was talking, she floated the theory it was maybe only gibberish instead.

"A hodgepodge," she told us. "She might be deranged."

"Still want her sleeping at your house?" Rowdy asked me.

What could I do but nod and tell him, "Yep"?

Besa insisted on crawling under the dinette table and dozed off with Bootsy in the crook of her leg while I did a fair bit of lying awake and getting up to look in on her since I'd gone and let Sheriff Rowdy poison the girl some in my head.

Worse still, I'd let myself run out of coffee, so come morning there was nothing but Sanka that Salvador had quite a lot to say about.

Ray rolled up with his donkey in his truck, not in the bed but on the king cab back seat. Her big, dusty head was hanging out of the window like she was just an oversized gun dog.

"How'd you get her in there?" Salvador wanted to know.

"Asked her nice. Then kicked her."

Ray had decided, upon seeing my cows, that his jenny would probably be best with me, and once he got the donkey out of his truck, he put the rest of us in it.

"Got a guy we need to see," he told us. "A Russian who speaks a lot of stuff. Lives down by the bay. Used to be some kind of spook. Temperamental, I'm told."

Now there's a word that can mean almost anything, from irritable to psychotic. I had to suspect a temperamental Russian spook would be on the felony end of things.

An hour in, we stopped for food at a barbecue joint even though it was shy of lunchtime. Ray was loathe to inflict a hungry Besa on some man he didn't actually know, so we loaded her up on chopped pork shoulder, corn dodgers, and red slaw.

"Cops would take care of her," Ray told us as we watched Besa eat. "Isn't like y'all need to do all this."

That was a thing I'd tossed and turned on. She'd just happened to pick my door, and I wasn't in the habit of getting roped into other people's trouble, but Besa seemed more helpless than your ordinary human, weak and foreign and put upon, and there was something about the way she curled up on my linoleum that got to me.

Salvador saved me the bother of explaining when he told Ray, "Feels like we do."

Ray's Russian lived on a boat, not a proper houseboat but some kind of industrial barge that had long since been abandoned. It wasn't even in the water but just sitting on a patch of marshy muck and pitched over maybe twenty degrees.

We had to walk up a pair of two by eights to get onto the deck. The entire vessel was an active and open opportunity for tetanus and looked to be held together by a blend of rust and seagull shit.

Ray smacked on the deckhouse sheeting with the flat of his hand. "Anybody here?" He slapped again. "Hello."

Besa saw him first. He was up on the roof looking over the edge down at us. She pointed and told us something. We all glanced up. He was shirtless and hairy and appeared to be wearing welder's glasses.

"Anthony sent me," Ray told him.

He said a thing back with no volume much and kept looking our way from behind his smoky lenses.

"Want us to come up?" Ray asked.

He grunted and withdrew.

We could soon hear him clanging down a ladder and then clomping down a staircase on the backside of the deckhouse. He was a hell of a sight once he finally stepped entirely into view. Sneakers with the toes cut out, greasy cargo shorts, and most everything else was a blend of primate fur and yellow paint, the sparkly kind they use on roadways. He was splattered all over with it.

"It's Pavel, right?" Ray asked.

He nodded and dropped his welder's glasses to dangle around his neck.

"Anthony call you?"

Pavel squinted and thought. He came out at length with, "Maybe."

He was Russian sure enough, had one of those cinematic, politburo accents.

"He said you might could translate for us."

Before Pavel could ask Ray, "Translate what?" Besa saved him the trouble by launching into an extended bit of business.

Pavel listened and then talked back. Besa had plenty more to tell him. It certainly sounded like they were having an authentic conversation.

"What's she speaking?" Ray asked.

"Romanian, sort of," Pavel told him.

"Sort of?"

Pavel held up a hand to shush Ray and then said something elaborate to Besa who told him a brief, concise thing right back.

"She's from Ungheni."

Even Salvador didn't know where that was.

"Moldova," Pavel said. "They talk Romanian. Some Russian. Some Gagauz. Like that."

"How'd she get here?" I asked him.

I got a spot of squinty consideration. "You brought her."

"Not here here. Here."

Pavel spoke briefly to Besa who spoke at length to Pavel back.

"Flew from Chisinau. Come for job."

"What job?" Ray wanted to know, and Pavel nearly dredged up the words to ask Besa all about it but decided instead to say to Ray along with the rest of us, "Tea?"

He'd built a level floor inside his tilted deckhouse, which made me about half dizzy once Pavel had waved us in. It was like one of those hillbilly theme park attractions where water runs uphill. I just leaned against the wall and tried not to pay much notice to the angles and the pitch until I could figure out where level was.

That left me with the decor to soak in, and I guess I'll call it eclectic since that seems to be the polite way to say 'a bunch of crap'. He had tools all over, including two jackhammers and the sort of diamond saw you could cut any damn thing with.

Pavel had furniture too, some of it built-in from back when his boat was seagoing, but he'd collected a half dozen yard chairs that he'd scattered about as well. He also owned a big brass samovar for making proper tea, and he even had a set of china for serving — cracked and stained china certainly, but it looked to have been nice once.

Pavel served us potent black tea and butter cookies dumped onto a plate. Then he yanked a stool out from somewhere and plopped himself down on it, just him in his dangling welding glasses and his cargo shorts and toeless sneakers. The rest was body hair, splattered paint, and folds of flesh. He hardly looked like a former spook. Pavel seemed more the guy who rides in the middle seat of the moving truck and gets stuck with the heavy end of everything.

"Tell him," was the full extent of Ray's instructions to me, so I filled Pavel in on how Besa had shown up and all we'd been through since.

"What job did she come for?" Ray asked.

Pavel put the question to Besa who had a mouthful of cookies. We waited. She swallowed and then told Pavel quite a lot of something in a lively and animated way.

"Exciting opportunity," Pavel told us, "in expanding technical field."

"When did she get here?" Ray wanted to know.

Pavel asked Besa. She gave him a matter-of-fact reply.

"Two weeks, maybe."

"How'd she end up in a root cellar?" Ray wanted to know.

Pavel quizzed Besa who rattled on at him, but by way of translation, he only told us, "Cannot say."

Then Pavel poured us all a second round of tea as he told Besa, "Biscuits kaput."

He turned the plate over. I made a mental note. That seemed like a useful technique.

3

I'd been living in a well-trampled rut for a while, out of choice and habit for sure, but that didn't make it any less dreary, so a mystery girl washing in and playing some havoc seemed pretty welcome to me.

I'd long since made my peace with the company of dogs and men and had never really known the itch to chase around after women. I was the sort inclined to wait for my charms to get discovered, and if they didn't, well there was Bootsy and Jack the lab before her and Buck the Australian shepherd before him along with a herd of cows to see to and a tractor to tinker with.

The few people who'd known me for a while were aware of my intended. Back years ago we'd done everything but book the church. From the outside, it looked like she'd taken up with a guy she'd met at work, so I got most of the sympathy, and she got most of the scowls, but in truth I'd dithered long enough to finally send her browsing. I see her sometimes out and around, and we're pleasant to each other. She catches me up on her kids, and I tell her stuff that makes me seem all right.

I ended up with dogs and farm work, so I was in a good spot to grouse about a foreign girl moving into my house while at the same having need for it. The companionship mattered. Even the fractured conversation. It wasn't much as relationships go, but it beat me and Bootsy on the sofa watching some mess on TV.

Salvador made a point of teaching me a little Romanian, and we took turns giving Besa spontaneous flatware coaching, but she had fingers for what she needed and couldn't see much point in a fork.

"Where does she come from," I asked Salvador more than once, "that people eat like that?"

Besa would hunch over her plate and shovel in her food with her thumb and her first two fingers and was so adept at it that she had to have been doing it all her life.

Salvador scoured the internet and told me all about the Moldovan boondocks, places near the Balanesti Mountains where folks lived poor and close to the ground.

We tried to keep things normal, me and Salvador. We had barn improvements we'd already hauled the lumber for, so we started in the way we'd gamed out and intended while Besa took an interest in housework. She'd caught sight of my string mop and had gone entirely giddy for it. It was a fancy, newish mop with a wringer built onto it, and Besa had launched into raptures over the thing, so I'd brought out the Mr. Clean and let her know she could mop what she liked. We could hear her dragging furniture around from all the way out at the barn.

"What's she doing?" Salvador wanted to know.

"Swabbing stuff," I told him.

"What stuff?"

"Hard to say." But that wasn't quite the case. It was easy to say. She was mopping pretty much everything.

My possessions all ended up smelling better while looking noticeably worse, but Besa seemed happy in her work, so I just left her to it.

Me and Salvador were tearing out stalls in the barn and putting in fresh feed bins with Ray's donkey as an active overseer. That jenny had a gift for finding a spot to stand where she was sure to be in our way. So the work was going like my work usually does, which is to say haltingly and poorly, when Sheriff Rowdy rolled up in his county prowler, climbed out and put his hat on. He checked himself in his side window and preened for a time in the drive.

I'd been expecting him or at least somebody official. They'd left us alone for a fair few days and them with a murdered guy to account for and a live girl to identify.

"Boys," the sheriff said once he'd joined us in the barn. He found a spot where he could lean to best effect. He plucked a cigarette out of his shirt pocket and fooled with it in a cowboy way as he glanced toward my back door. "She in there?"

I nodded.

Sheriff Rowdy lit his cigarette. Blue, acrid smoke. A Pall Mall. "Ray said something about a Russian on a boat somewhere."

I let Salvador nod this time.

"How'd that go?"

"She's from Moldova," I told the Sheriff. "Came over here for some kind of job."

"Say how she got locked up?"

I shook my head. "Not exactly."

"Name on the dead guy's a phony," Sheriff Rowdy told us. "Whole thing's peculiar." He puffed and thought. "So Moldovan's what she's talking?"

"Romanian," Salvador told him. "Fellow said that's what they speak over there."

Sheriff Rowdy wasn't about to get educated by a Mexican. He shook his head and spat like he was just the sort of man who'd insist on talking Moldovan in Moldova

Just then, Besa stepped out the back door to shoot a bucket of filthy water into the yard before chattering at us briefly and ducking back into the house.

"Wouldn't have her under my roof," the sheriff told me, "knowing what little we know."

That brand of misgiving had crossed my mind as well. It cropped up usually at about half past three in the a.m. when I do most of my pitching around. I couldn't truly know if Besa was all right or not. She was still sleeping under my kitchen table and still eating six or eight meals a day, and I'd entirely failed to persuade her to leave off mopping my living room carpet.

She called me 'meester' every now and again and said sometimes 'no' and 'yes', but she mostly came out with foreign talk as she ate with only her fingers. One night I dreamed she was standing by my bed with a boning knife.

We didn't see much of Ray. He finally swung by a few days after Sheriff Rowdy's visit, but it turned out he didn't have anything to tell us, had mostly come to check on his donkey.

"Isn't like I'd hand her off to get treated any old way."

When I pressed him for a crumb, all he'd say was, "Working on it." Then Ray inspected the improvements we'd made on the barn. The new corn crib. New trough. Easy-draining parlor floor.

"Hell, boys," he told us, "I'd be a cow in here."

By then I was half ready to believe there was nothing complicated to know and that Besa would soon get collected and sent back home. I was going to end up with some moldy rugs, a donkey, and no crackers.

Then Bootsy barked one evening, and I soon had a knock at the door. I opened it to a woman who was the type of creature you almost never see out where I live. Willowy tall and fashionably dressed in snug jeans and a blouse. Boots that looked pricey and a haircut that looked it too.

"Hi," she said. "I think I'm lost." She had an envelope in her hand.

There was a guy in a sedan out in the drive. I could see him from the neck down. He looked a lot less swanky. "Odd pair, these two" was what flashed through my head.

"I'm looking for a Joseph Richardson," she said and held out her envelope.

"Know a Danny." I unlatched the screen door and pushed it open. She handed the envelope to me. It was empty and unsealed, and there was nothing written on it anywhere.

By the time I glanced up, she had something in her hand that looked to me like a flashlight. She reached over and touched me with it, and my evening took a turn.

I've since been schooled in the difference between your basic taser and stun gun, and I've had the physiological effects of raw voltage explained to me at some length by Deputy Gwen who turned out to be kind of a hobbyist.

"Couldn't move at all, could you?" I remember she asked me.

"Just my bowels," I said.

I could remember hearing Besa scream before I smacked my head on the floor and went cloudy. Lucky for me, I was in the living room where the rug was fluffed and sudsy, so I only got a bump and some soap in my ears.

Bootsy was still growling by the time I could sit up, and Besa wasn't anywhere around.

I called Ray first. He came straight over, and I tried to tell him every little thing I could remember. About the woman. About the sedan. The man at the wheel. The flashlight.

"Accent?"

"Regular. A little upper crusty maybe."

"Age?"

"Thirty-something. Really put together. Guy in the car looked kind of low-rent. Blue. Maybe a Dodge."

"Ever been zapped before?" Ray wanted to know.

I shook my head.

"Be a whole lot worse tomorrow."

I got invited to come by the PD for a proper statement, but they didn't seem too interested in any of it. A foreign girl they'd failed to properly identify had been whisked away by people they seemed to doubt they'd ever find, so they could go back to their bar fights and their traffic violations.

Come morning, I enlisted Salvador to help me start in on the brand of looking I knew I'd have to do. I was gimpy from having gotten zapped. My joints all ached and my muscles too, and I'd only made it as far as the dinette table by the time Salvador had arrived.

"What's Ray say?" he asked me.

"Nothing much. Let's you and me go around to her spots and try to put this thing together. Maybe start at that cow farm, just work through every damn thing."

"If that's what you want. You feeling up to it?"

I wasn't really but said I was.

"I got zapped once," Salvador told me on the way. "Couldn't pee for the best part of a week."

"Not one of my complaints. Though my tongue sort of itches."

"I had something like that. My hair hurt."

We had to park on the roadside just like before and walk the rutted, pitchy track up to that abandoned belted-galloway house. Salvador found a busted shovel handle for me to use as a kind of staff. Even still, I had to take a break halfway up to let my legs recover, and I was done in by the time we reached the place.

It was just like we'd seen it before with the front door standing half open. Salvador climbed up onto the porch and went inside for a snoop around. He came out with the calendar I'd seen hanging on the front room wall. The funeral home it advertised had long been out of business. Somebody'd had a hair appointment in September of '96.

We circled the house expecting to see the same mess we'd seen already, but the cellar where Besa had been shut up didn't look the way we'd left it. There was a plank across the bulkhead doors with a bunch of twenty-penny nails driven through it. Somebody had closed that cellar up tight and meant for it to stay that way.

"Rowdy and them?" I asked Salvador, and that's when the pounding started. The grunting and the yelling, the howling from inside.

"Got a bar in the Jeep," he told me and went hustling to get it.

"Just hold on," I barked toward the cellar doors, but the racket didn't quit. It kept up even once Salvador had started working on that plank. We finally got the thing pried loose enough to partly open one of the doors, and the creature inside came wriggling out. We knew him straightaway.

It was the kid with the slop bucket. The one with the Suzuki who'd taken a pot shot at us. He wasn't so dirty we couldn't recognize him, but it was a close-run thing. He was wearing just underpants and was caked in cellar grime and filth.

The boy bathed us in teen gratitude the moment he'd caught his breath. He hooked his hair behind his ears and told us, "About damn time."

He wouldn't say anything else at first beyond, "Get the law. I don't care."

"Who we calling?" Salvador wanted to know. "Going to be Ray or Rowdy?"

Ray came straight over and found us. He even brought a friend. Ray jabbed his thumb at his companion, a handsome raw-boned lady with a shiner. "Kate," he told us.

We got a head jerk from her.

Salvador, ever curious, pointed at her puffy eye.

"Fuckwit. Elbow." Kate seemed to be on a faster loop than Ray, but she sure had his sense of economy.

Ray asked the kid, "What do they call you?"

The boy went sullen and sweary.

"Let me see that." Ray grabbed my shovel handle.

"Go on. Hit me. I don't care."

Ray obliged him.

"Shit! Ow!"

"What's your name?"

"Curtis."

"Who put you in that hole?"

Curtis shrugged. "Some boys."

"Who?" Ray asked.

Curtis shrugged again.

"How long you been in there?"

"What's today?"

We helped Curtis work out that he'd been locked in that cellar for just shy of three days.

"What boys?" Ray wanted to know.

Curtis shrugged another time. Ray couldn't be bothered to raise the shovel handle and so just swatted the kid with his open hand.

That passed for surprising, coming from Ray. Almost any lively, decisive thing was surprising coming from Ray. Even Curtis seemed shocked, which was probably the point.

"We was out at the farm, messing around," Curtis said.

"Farm with the goat?"

"Naw." Curtis country pointed in the general direction of Neptune.

"Go with this lady here," Ray told him. "You're going to take us there."

Curtis failed to budge for a moment, so Kate kicked him crisply in the backside. Like teenage boys will, he got both pitiful and half erect together.

"Move," Kate said, and Curtis slouched off with her giving him the odd shove, driving him down toward the road and Ray's truck.

"I say we hold off on Rowdy," Ray suggested to me and Salvador. "I'd like to get the bigger picture before they weigh in and screw it up."

That was fine with us, and me and Salvador nodded while Curtis wailed from down along the track. From where I stood it looked very much like Kate had pinched his nipple.

"She some kind of cop?" I asked Ray.

He nodded.

"She here to help us with Besa?"

Curtis shrieked.

"Already on it," Ray said.

We followed Ray in the Cherokee. It was slow going all the way. First, we went back out to the blacktop and then down dirt roads and around. I didn't say a lot because my muscles were tender and my joints all ached, so I was just working to get comfortable and failing at it as we went, which Salvador decided to take for something other than it was.

The man has convinced himself he has a gift for reading people, and he soon felt like he knew precisely where my trouble might reside.

"Hear me on this," he started in. "Don't go blaming yourself about Besa. She was into this mess before she ever showed up at your door, and how are you going to know that woman from yesterday's got a zapper?"

"Couldn't know," I told him, "and I don't blame myself."

"*Exactement*," Salvador said and treated me to his earnest cable melodrama look.

Salvador had picked up most of his Americana off the television, and he'd go showy sincere when he wanted to chew on a thing. That's how they did it on the sorts of evening dramas Salvador liked to watch, and somebody on one of them must have been partial to "Hear me on this" and "*Exactement*".

I figured a surgeon on one of those medical shows because whenever Salvador went earnest, I half expected to get the troubling results of a biopsy back.

Ray's truck turned down a rutted track. I couldn't begin to say where we were. There were metal buildings up ahead or shipping containers or something.

The place we'd arrived at looked to have been a proper farm of some size. The metal outbuildings proved to be bulk barns, big containers where the burly had been cured. There were a couple of stick-built sheds as well.

Curtis was giving Ray and Kate an accounting of the place by the time me and Salvador reached them.

"He says they kept them here," Ray told us. "Sounds like seven or eight women."

"For what?" I asked.

"Says he isn't sure." That from Kate. "Don't you?"

Curtis looked at the ground and shrugged.

Kate grabbed a nipple and gave it a twist. Curtis yelped and got erect again.

We noticed, us guys, and sympathized with the boy as best we could. "I went through about a year like that," Ray confessed to me and Salvador. "1983. Millie Reston. Birthmark on her left thigh. I got to see it all of twice."

Kate did some more nipple twisting, and Curtis whined but stayed aroused, even after Kate had delivered a mighty flick to Curtis' manhood, which he seemed content to catalog as 'touched finally by a girl!'.

"Shaped like Indiana," Ray told us. "She's got an Etsy store now. I bought three pairs of baby socks. I don't even know any babies."

That was like a memoir, coming from Ray.

"How about we walk him around," Kate suggested.

We all nodded, and Kate shoved Curtis.

We closed on the nearest bulk barn. Both its doors were shut and latched.

"Open it," Kate said.

Curtis unlatched a door and swung it wide, but there was nothing inside beyond the sweet scent of cured burley. Curtis swung open the carriage door on one of the stick-built sheds. Empty too but for old farm junk.

"You work on this farm?" Ray asked him.

Curtis nodded. "Fed them and shot them sometimes with the hose."

We were walking to the last barn, the largest one. Its main door had fallen off the runners and was laying in the weeds.

"Nothing much in there," Curtis said and then conspicuously hung back.

Ray and Kate went on in while me and Salvador stayed outside with Curtis.

"I ain't done none of this," he told us. "Just fed them and shot them with the hose."

Ray stepped back out and motioned us all in.

An old field wagon missing a wheel was parked inside against the near wall. It had luggage on it, what looked like ten or twelve bags, and there was some kind of jackleg cage in a corner — rabbit wire and spruce planks — about ten feet across.

"Curtis?" was all Ray said.

"I ain't done none of this."

"None of what exactly?"

Ray opened a sky-blue overnight bag. There was a woman's underthings in it. A pouch full of makeup. A coiled white belt.

Curtis told us again that he'd just fed them and shot them with the hose.

Kate was all for pummeling Curtis, chiefly for being a country fool, which Curtis stayed semi-hard about.

The sheriff's gang showed up in straggling force and took turns asking us all the same questions, especially Curtis who did quite a lot of staring at the ground. When Sheriff Rowdy arrived and set about quizzing me and Salvador, I made a point of staying mum so Salvador could do the talking since Sheriff Rowdy had a way of looking gassy when Mexicans told him stuff.

"This all they do?" Salvador asked me once we were back in his Jeep. He worked his way past two crime scene trucks and about a half-dozen cruisers. "Just fool around and figure nothing out?"

What could I tell the man, other than, *"Exactement."*

We went through the motions with Rowdy's bunch. I went through them anyway while Salvador pled Mexican and stuck with barn repairs. For his part, Ray stopped in to trade insults with the sheriff. I know because I was sitting there in the room when he arrived. I was answering more questions I'd answered already when Ray stepped in from the hallway and helped himself to a chair.

As interrogation rooms go, the local PD had an attractive sort. A decent enough table with a couple of stout and galvanized eye hooks in it, and somebody had hung photos of various local attractions on the three unmirrored walls. A nice view of the Little Bug Island River, a sunset shot of the old slate pit out toward Rowden, and a flyover look at the college in Dempsey where they've got a grove of maples and a gloomy gothic church.

Ray started in making the case for why Sheriff Rowdy was wasting my time and suggested alternative avenues of legitimate inquiry.

That had the effect of touching off a lively round of bickering between Ray and Rowdy that presently found its way (like most all their quarrels) back to "Meekins and them."

I only knew a murder-suicide had gone to murder-murder and that Ray and Rowdy appeared to have tangled over it ever since.

"What happened exactly?" I asked them both once they'd left a gap for me to do it.

"Go on," Rowdy said. "Tell him."

"Case went wrong," Ray said. "We both worked in Georgia once."

"Wrong how?"

"I got involved with a witness," Ray told me. "Kind of clouded my judgement."

"Witness?" Rowdy had a hoot about that.

"Is she Meekins?" I asked.

"Naw," Rowdy told me. "Meekins was one of the dead guys. She was hooked up with the other one. Married, wasn't she?" he asked Ray.

"Engaged."

"Right. Had the ring and all." Ray was doing his glacial, deliberate thing, so Sheriff Rowdy gave the man a poke. "Tell him."

"She played me," Ray said. "I was a sad case back then." He seemed to remember I'd been in his house, had seen his stuff, and so he added, "Sadder."

Then he told me the story with Sheriff Rowdy occasionally throwing in. They were working midnights out near Dahlonega, not partners but just sharing shifts, when they both got dispatched to see a civilian about gunshots in the small hours.

"Georgia, you know?" Ray said. "Who figured it'd be anything?"

"The shooting came from a big old estate house," Rowdy told me. "Out there by the lake."

"Hung back for maybe a quarter hour," Ray informed me. "Didn't hear anything, and the old bird who'd called it in was kind of a regular complainer."

"Don't want to roll up on money and be wrong." That from Sheriff Rowdy.

They finally decided to walk up, straight across the lawn to the house that they could see was all lit on the bottom. They were thinking it'd be a couple of fellows full of single malt with a pistol, so they eased in quiet and dark and were looking to get out just the same if they came across some lubricated swell showing off his Desert Eagle.

"Turned out different," Ray said. "Dead guy in the house. Another one on the back porch. Multiple gunshots for the inside guy. One in the mouth outside."

"Amanda, wasn't it?"

Ray exhaled. "You know it was."

"Dead one on the porch was her intended."

"I went out to notify her," Ray said.

"Just him," Rowdy told me like maybe I ought to weigh that as Ray talked.

Ray described her house. The sedan in the drive. The bull terrier that charged out from under a bush or somewhere to greet him.

"I was on the roof of my Crown Vic when she came out and called him off."

Ray described her, this Amanda, but not in a vivid and personal way. More like you might describe a glimpse of

Bigfoot. According to Ray, she was blue-eyed brunette about five eight, medium build.

Ray said she took the news poorly. The woman collapsed onto the front lawn and so turned loose of her dog's collar, which put Ray back on the roof of his car.

"I wasn't going to shoot him," Ray said. "She had a dead fiancee already, but she just kept rolling around and blubbering, so I came down and got bit twice." Ray rolled up a pants leg and showed me his scars. "Worked the dog into the cruiser and shut the door. Called an ambulance for her and one for me. Ended up with seventeen stitches."

"Get to it," Rowdy told him.

"She came to see me at my house, brought flowers and cake. Stayed for a while, and we just talked and stuff. I checked on her a day or two later. She came back and checked on me. I was just trying to comfort the woman, honest to God, but things got out of hand. Hard to say why. I sure knew better, but I wasn't in a good way back then."

"Murder-murder?" I asked Ray.

"We had a tech down there . . ."

"Carlton," the sheriff said.

"Carlton always got a twitch," Ray told me, "when stuff didn't quite add up."

Carlton, as it turned out, didn't like a couple of the details. They weren't wrong or damning exactly, but they seemed slightly out of true. Something to do with a break in the splatter on the porch. Something to do with the angle of entry.

"We got a warrant on the girlfriend," Rowdy said, "and Carlton found some blood inside her front door lock. Like she'd had some on her key when it went in."

"Boyfriend's?"

Rowdy and Ray both nodded.

"Took a plea," Rowdy told me. "They've got her down in Metro State."

"I guess people'll surprise you." I said that a lot, but I don't think I've ever quite meant it, or maybe I meant that people could let the air out of just about any damn thing.

"That's it? That's why you two are so scratchy?"

"Naw," Sheriff Rowdy told me. "We just don't like each other much."

That they could agree about. Ray touched his nose and nodded.

Besa had only been gone a couple of days when more pounding woke me up. I went to the closet, fetched my rifle, shouted at the front door, "What?"

I got some words back I couldn't make out, threw the bolt, and there she was.

Besa was wearing a gentleman's dress shirt and just underpants otherwise. It was the kind of shirt with the collar one color and the rest of the thing another like a banker or a TV lawyer might wear. It would have been a real nice item, except for all the blood.

Kate

1

I tried to sell it as a bad reflex, just one of those odd, stray things that happens when a guy you're arresting swings around and elbows you in the eye. Your foot might fly up and catch his crotch. You might flail blindly and slug him. And he could easily bang his head on your knee in the middle of collapsing. That sort of cascading calamity must happen all the time.

To his credit, the boss let me get it all out and even appeared to be favoring me with sympathetic attention. He did shift a few of the family photos on his desk while I was talking. He had a new one of his wife in a party dress. She looked a bit gym ravaged, and I couldn't help but notice his middle boy had that dire teen thing going on — half sneer, half godawful hair.

"His brother," Wilcox told me, "got the whole thing on his phone."

I watched me catch an elbow and then get pissed and reflex all over the guy.

"Oh."

"Yeah. Oh.

Naturally, Wilcox had plenty to say about the man hours I'd cost the unit. He'd reviewed my history of reflex trouble over my twelve years at the Bureau and so could cite impetuous episodes in chronological order.

"Jesus, LeComte," he said at last, "I thought you'd outgrow this by now."

"Guess I'm just enthusiastic, sir."

"So's Becky." He picked up a framed photo and showed me a snapshot of his latest beagle.

"I was defending myself. Might have overdone it."

Wilcox exhaled and clicked his pen while I tried to decide what kind of man would name a beagle Becky.

"You're taking a leave," he told me and shoved a document my way. He offered his pen. "Three months, unpaid. Best I could get. They want to cut you loose upstairs."

Our neighbor had owned a wolfhound named Uriah once, but he was an actuary and a full-blown Dickens nerd. Becky was what you called your angelfish if you were six.

"Thank you, sir." I signed in two spots.

The boss offered his hand, and I took it. I gave him my office smile. I nodded. I already knew I'd drop in on Ray, wherever exactly he was.

We had a thing, me and Ray. It might have been intermittent, but it was reliably ongoing and didn't depend on either one of us checking in and catching up. I remember back when I was working in Philly for a month, I came out of the field office to find Ray sitting in the plaza on Arch. He hadn't called or texted or anything. He'd just caught the train from somewhere.

It was one of our usual sorts of reunions. We told each other, "Hey."

That time he stayed for the best part of a week. He was in between jobs, not at all unusual for Ray because he has a way of getting itchy, giving his notice, and taking off. And I want to be clear — the charm of the man isn't his stinginess with palaver. It's more that Ray is distilled and concentrated every way you can be. In speech, in deed, in principles — he's reduced it all to an elixir.

The problem was I didn't know exactly where he'd gone. Ray had moved twice since I'd last seen him, and he'd told me he'd taken his brother in. His name was Doug or Dan or something, and though they'd not fallen out exactly, they'd never been anything like close. Doug/Dan was married with kids, and he'd had a settled life until he'd dropped it all for some woman from work, and then she'd wearied of him. He was tapped out and unemployed, estranged from most everybody by the time he got diagnosed.

Ray housed and nursed his brother, kept the drugs flowing and the pain at bay once they'd given up on treatment. I got the thrust of it all in one brief phone call when Ray dialed me out of the blue. Having to watch his brother die was dredging up a lot of stuff, and Ray went on about it for nearly half an hour because, wherever he was, he'd not located anybody else he could tell.

I sat around my apartment for three days after my dismissal before I texted Ray. Then I waited nearly a week for him to get back with directions. I took that as his way of saying, "All right. Come on. I guess."

Even with directions, I had a hell of a time locating him because Ray was back in one of those Allegheny valleys regular civilization hasn't quite reached. The roads had once been numbered and marked, but the locals had seen fit to knock down all the signs, so I did a lot of stopping at junctions and failing to get a signal, even sought directions from a man at a dumpster who was fishing for treasure instead of putting stuff in.

I finally popped out on a blacktop and drove maybe six miles to a Hardee's where I got enough signal to dial Ray. After maybe half an hour he showed.

"Jesus," was what I told him the moment he walked in.

Ray took my meaning — he always does — and said back, "He's not here."

Ray was living in his usual variety of farmhouse, just a bit more isolated and run down. The place was cheap, and since Ray wasn't working in any regular way, he didn't need to be near anywhere. There was still sick brother stuff in the spare room, a couple of robes and pajamas on a door hook and a rolling rack where the drug bags hung.

"Yeah," Ray said when he caught me looking at the paint-by-numbers Matterhorn over the bed. "We did that before he got bad. Pretty awful, isn't it?"

And I do believe that was about the extent of the dead brother talk between us. Ray supplied me with a skimpy version of how he'd ended up where he was. He'd worked a stint down on the coast I hadn't known a thing about and then had taken a security gig with some outfit near Knoxville.

"Stored platinum," Ray told me. "Little pellets from catalytic converters. They were worried about thieves, but you'd have needed a crane to pick the damn stuff up."

We were in bed at that moment, and I was working to snag Ray's attention. He's a decent goer when you can get him to focus on the job.

"I read all of Wilkie Collins," he told me. "Can't say I'm better for it."

In the weeks before I found him, Ray had taken on a job the local police couldn't be bothered with.

"It's a good one," he told me at lunch over one of his nasty stews. This was the chicken and turnip version that I'd complimented him on one time, not lavishly or even sincerely, but he's made it for me ever since. It's usually brown and tart and thick like porridge. Ray serves it on toast underneath shredded cheese that you'd think might help but doesn't.

"So this girl shows up," he started in. Ray told me where and how and then ticked off assorted curious particulars about her.

"Hold on. What dead guy?"

Ray described where he found the body and then touched his neck on either side. "Clean as you like. Emptied him right out. Ever seen anything like that?"

I actually had and nodded. "Bergen County. Filipino gang. Real stabby and flashy about it."

"They'd kind of stick out around here."

"What's the girl say?"

"She's not around to ask."

He filled me in on what had happened to her.

"She was living with this farmer?"

Ray nodded. "He seems decent enough. All I know is my donkey's happy."

"Is that some kind of cornpone saying?"

Ray thought for a moment. "Is now."

Just then, Ray's phone rang, and it was the farmer himself, Whit. Him and a buddy had decided to tour around and do some reinvestigating and had turned up a witness and marginal accomplice they wanted Ray to come and see.

"You don't have to go," he told me.

"Like hell." Anything to get away from that damn stew.

So I met Whit and Salvador and scraggly Curtis in his filthy undershorts. Women excited Curtis, any woman just hanging around being female, so my shiner didn't much matter as long as I pawed the boy and crowded close.

Once the county PD had quizzed him, Curtis popped out cleanly to us, and Ray made sure I was out in the lot to meet him with my blouse half undone. That was Ray's suggestion, but I knew Curtis didn't require a come on. I could brush his arm and make it a bit of a chore for him to walk.

I drove Curtis to Bojangles where I bought him a three-wing dinner and then bought it again and, while he ate, heard him out with my best approximation of girlish sympathy.

"They didn't feed me nothing," Curtis kept saying. He was mystified and insulted that no deputy had gone to the bother to give him even a pack of nabs. "I was locked in a damn hole. What the hell's wrong with people?"

I had a noise for that and made it as I laid my hand on his arm.

Curtis immediately reached to adjust himself. I was old enough to be his mother and had a puffy, elbowed eye, but I was right next to Curtis and anatomically correct.

"What did you tell them?" I asked him. I kept my hand just where it was.

"You know. Stuff."

I wiped Curtis' greasy mouth with a napkin and giggled. "You're a mess."

He blushed and caught the eye of a man across the way, a black gentleman in a straw fedora.

"What are you looking at?" Curtis shouted.

I squeezed his arm. "What am I going to do with you?"

Curtis twitched. Curtis flushed. He muttered, "I don't know."

Curtis was like most men, just the remedial version, so it wasn't much of a challenge to nudge and steer him where I wanted him to go. I bought Curtis cigarettes after he'd finished his supper, and we ended up at a junky, trash-strewn park with a lake shaped like a butter bean right in the middle of it. The water was scummy, and a truck tire broke the surface on the far side.

"I need to know what you know." I tried to say it in such a way as to make the whole enterprise sound vaguely lascivious and tantric.

We were sitting on a picnic table, and Curtis was smoking, hooding his butt with his hand. I'd sidled as close as I could and waited for Curtis to go properly squirmy. He was on the way to it when my phone rang. I dug it out and checked it, huffed one time, said, "Ray" and dismissed the call.

"He your boyfriend or something?"

"Was once. Won't let it go."

My phone rang again. Ray. I killed the call, which raised a smile from Curtis.

"Where's your girl?"

Curtis flicked his smoke and gave me a look. "Maybe right here," he said. And the pimply son-of-a-bitch went for me with both hands.

"Easy."

I couldn't tell at first just what he might be after, didn't know if it was clumsy romance or something a bit more dire. He cleared that up by punching me hard in the gut one time. Then he caught me a shot to my good eye, so I reached for the gun I didn't have, the mace I wasn't carrying, which were both sitting on Ray's dresser because it was just Curtis after all.

I managed to juke and shift enough to take a glancing jab to the arm.

"Curtis."

"Shut up!"

He tried a haymaker that missed everything. Instead of fighting back, I worked to keep the picnic table between us.

"Y'all think I'm stupid."

He pretty much had me there. "We just want the girl back. Figured you could help us."

"Told you already. Don't know about no girl."

With that, Curtis dove straight across the table and somehow managed to marry tackling me with copping a thorough feel, so I got groped and knocked over backward into that greasy bean-shaped pond. Curtis sat on me and held me under until he'd grabbed my ass sufficiently to come away with my keys.

Then he stood up and kicked me twice and went running toward the lot. He was gone by the time I'd found the breath to crawl out of the water.

My phone was doused and ruined. I smelled like a sump hole. My wet jeans had chafed me raw before I'd even reached the road.

When Ray couldn't get me on the phone, he'd gone out in his truck to look, so he found me before I'd walked more than half a mile. My history with Ray — the casework part — was informed here and there by me free-lancing against Ray's stated instructions and then him coming along behind me to tidy up. He'd always advise me to listen to him in future, and I'd always promise I would. It was what we had instead of matrimony.

Ray filled his bathtub for me.

"This all you got?" I held up Ray's bar of dollar-store soap. "I'm not really looking for pumice action."

"He's fifteen, right? And he ends up with your car?"

What could I say? I shrugged. "Thought his woody would slow him down."

"I've got dish soap and some dandruff shampoo."

"Shampoo, I guess." Ray fetched it for me, the blue kind in a tube.

Ray pointed out a coming bruise on my rib cage.

"Yeah, caught me a good one." I had a lather going on my inflamed thighs by then. "How's my eye look?"

"Like your other one."

"Do my back, duckie?"

Because he's Ray, he took the tube and did.

2

They found my car in the middle school lot, and some musclehead deputy tried to charge me two hundred dollars for towing and impound, but sheriff hop-a-long wouldn't hear of it.

"Professional courtesy," he said as he made a show of ripping the paperwork up.

"Why are you even on this?" the sheriff wanted to know. He was talking to Ray, was the sort of man built to ignore a woman. "If she couldn't handle the boy, why let her pick him up?"

"She's standing right here," I said. "Sometimes things go sideways, you know?"

"Yeah. Maybe. I guess." The sheriff treated me to a tip-to-toe once over. "Want to file charges on him? Ray said he beat you up."

Ray, I felt sure, had never said any such thing, but I did have one shiner fading and another one coming on, so I probably looked like taking a punch was a going pastime for me.

"Or we could just find him," I suggested. "Who are his people? He must have family."

"We know his uncle pretty good." He was back to talking to Ray. "Did three years for arson. Time in county for simple assault, but that was all nearly a decade ago. Hasn't been through here since."

"How about that luggage?" I asked him.

"You know how it is," he said to Ray. "Short-handed and all."

"Mind if we have a look?" Ray asked.

The sheriff twitched, shrugged, didn't much care. He walked us deep into the PD and pointed down a stairwell.

"It's all back there past some chairs and mess. Do what you want," he told us.

All the suitcases and stuff we'd come across on that wagon in the barn was now sharing an unpainted block room with some file boxes and a furnace. Nothing about the way those bags were piled up suggested anybody had even opened one.

The contents were all clothes. Nothing but clothes. No personal papers. No travel documents. No receipts or ticket stubs or boarding passes. Just women's clothes and shoes. No jewelry even. Few toiletries. And the luggage tags had all been removed.

"I've got a Greek shirt label," Ray said.

"Russian or something over here, and some kind of Baltic cigarettes stuck in a shoe."

I showed Ray the bottom of a hard-sided bag where somebody had written a name in Sharpie, which we couldn't between us make out.

"Besa said she came for a job," Ray told me. "This is feeling kind of dark."

I knew why too. It was organized. Some son-of-a-bitch was thinking. You don't import people in batches unless you've got a plan.

"And out of all the stuff you don't like . . . ?"

Ray gave that some thought. "Dead guy, I guess, so far."

So we piled into Ray's truck and headed out to where Ray had found him.

"He didn't look like he fit the decor," Ray told me along the way. "His shoes were too nice. Better haircut than you see out in the county. Phony name on the ID they found. Got no idea who he is. "

I'm not at all sure how Ray settled on the route to get us where we were going because we drove along unmarked dirt tracks through the backwoods for six or eight miles. We crossed a stream twice, once on an actual bridge, and we passed a lot of rusty, half-standing wire fencing enclosing nothing but weedy ground and spindly trees.

After forty-five minutes Ray finally stopped in front of what looked more or less like a house. Rusted tin roof. Dormer windows. Mildewed asbestos shingles. A wealth of sticker bushes and trash all over the place.

The front door was nailed shut in what appeared to be a jackleg version of weather stripping, so we went around back and touched off some racket in the undergrowth. Eventually, a creature came out. It looked like some kind of failed pony.

"Hell," Ray said. "Rowdy promised they'd haul him off."

That beast might have been on the far side of the yard, but I could smell him well enough from where we were. He had a few strands of vine hanging from his mouth and mud up to his elbows, or knees, or whatever. He gave the impression of having once been white.

"What is that?"

"A goat," Ray told me. "Probably a Saanen."

Ray had a way of going pedantic where it came to stuff you didn't need details about.

"Swiss originally. Good milkers."

He must have heard us talking about him because that goat came right over with his head down and gave me a powerful shove.

"Hey!"

He shoved me another time.

"Do something," I told Ray.

"Just goat stuff," he said. Ray gazed around the property. "He's damn near cleared the yard." Ray grabbed that goat and gave him a push. "Go on." The creature more or less retired. Then Ray mounted the small rear stoop, tore through a strip of yellow police tape, shouldered the door open, and went on into the house.

It smelled like homicide in there. Quarts of spilled blood will do that. Of course, it also stank of must and rot and decades of cooking oil. I followed Ray into the kitchen.

"He was sitting over there."

I could see well enough the man's outline where all the dried blood wasn't. Ray showed me a photo of the guy's face on the screen of his phone.

Ray opened a cabinet door, and a plump mouse fell out. He sat on the countertop looking imposed upon and only waddled off after a bit.

"Hop along and them turn up anything in here?"

"Not that I've heard about."

So me and Ray did some scouring ourselves. We'd mounted that sort of search before and had developed a method, which put us in the same room at the same time, just circulating in different directions. Then we'd meet and pass and the other would hunt where the first one had already been.

We started in the front parlor, and the place struck me as weird in an archeological sort of way. It was like the furniture had already been in the house and in use by somebody when an entirely new bunch had taken over and lived on top of what was there.

We found, for instance, a half-dozen briar pipes and a couple of dried out bags of Burley & Bright. There was an industrial-sized nail clipper as well and a tub of off-brand petroleum jelly along with a balled up pair of compression stockings shoved between two sofa cushions.

"A lot of old-man stuff."

Ray nodded and held up a pair of reading glasses with one of the earpieces missing. There was a box of dusty fatwood by the fireplace and a pickle jar crammed with grocery coupons on the mantelpiece. Then on top of all that was more recent crap, mostly cans and cups and glasses, food wrappers, a half-eaten sack of jerky, a bunch of scratch-off lottery cards.

In the only bedroom downstairs, we found an entire wardrobe of coveralls and three pairs of work boots in various states of dilapidation. Upstairs, somebody had left a sleeping bag on one of the double beds, and Ray turned up a stomped

and busted USB key on the floor behind the upstairs toilet.

"Know who's on the deed?" I asked Ray.

He didn't and parked himself in a dormer to make a call

while I opened all the drawers I could and shifted the contents

around.

"Definitely tweaker shit on top of geezer stuff," I told

Ray once I'd circled back.

"The property belonged to a Warren Crater, deceased.

Natural causes, eight months ago."

"Any grieving relatives?"

Ray shook his head. "Estate's unclaimed."

"What are the chances somebody just happened onto this

place?" We were back in the kitchen by then.

"I'd say pretty low," Ray told me. "I live around here

and, you saw me, I had a hard time finding it twice."

We moved out of the kitchen and into the backyard as we

talked. That filthy goat came wandering up to join us, lowered

its head and had a go at Ray this time.

Ray Grabbed him by the ears. "Going to need your

help."

"Doing what?"

"Just don't stand right behind him."

You wouldn't think a goat would be up for a ride on the back seat of a king cab truck, but this particular specimen hung his head out the window and bleated in a merry sort of way. Of course, he chewed a bit of upholstery as well and ate about half a floor mat.

"I thought you just got rid of a donkey."

"Couldn't leave him out there," Ray said.

I'd never been around a goat and can't be sure this one was standard and normal, but, given the time for it, I'm persuaded he would have eaten Ray's truck interior down to the steel.

We ended up bathing that goat together because we were working on Ray's sort of case. Obscure motives, colorful participants, almost always livestock. I'd spent no little time trying to decide if Ray made things peculiar or if weird stuff just found him out because he was, you know, Ray.

When I met him, he was working a case touched off by a corpse up in a treetop, and then I'd given him some phone-in advice on a guy who specialized in pubic haircuts at gunpoint.

There was no sex involved, just grooming, and he always brought along a three-legged calico cat.

I can say when I drove down from D.C. I didn't expect to be shampooing a goat. Fortunately, that goat turned out to be eager for a bath and stood by placidly making goaty noises. He shook like a dog once we'd rinsed him down.

For a while there we didn't see Salvador or farmer Whit either one since Ray had precious little to tell them. Instead, we hiked and lazed, took the odd country ride, and we'd sit out evenings on Ray's porch drinking Ray's cheap bourbon and have the sort of conversations I usually had with Ray. Desultory doesn't quite cover it because they're skimpier than that.

"What if that girl's in a hole somewhere again?" I asked him in a regular way.

"She's not," was Ray's usual answer. "I'm thinking she's either dead or fine."

"Based on what?"

"You know." He'd tap his sternum.

Ray was trying to be less constipated, more improvisational and open to whim. It was the sort of thing he'd long paid lip service to, but Ray was naturally a grinder and couldn't just up and be spontaneous no matter what he said. I noticed, however, in the wake of his brother's death, he'd gone at least a little more lax.

Doug/Dan, the brother, was four years older than Ray and had worked as some kind of salesman. I met him once outside Roanoke when Ray was helping me with a warrant, and I didn't know he was Ray's brother until after he'd driven off. We were in a box-store parking lot keeping eyes on our guy when a shiny new SUV came rolling our way and stopped.

"Thought that was you," the driver said to Ray.

"You living here now?" Ray asked him.

"Salem," he said. "You?"

Ray gestured generally westward and told him only, "You know." Then he turned my way and said to the guy at the wheel, "Kate."

"Things all right?"

Ray nodded. "You?"

"Oh yeah."

Then they both said nothing until Ray chimed in with, "We're kind of working on something."

"Come around sometime."

Ray nodded. The man drove off, and we checked to make sure our guy's sedan was still sitting where we'd last seen it.

"Who was that?" I asked Ray after a while.

He said the last thing I'd expected to hear. "My big brother."

I'd fallen out with most of my people. My parents had moved to the Ozarks where my mother brewed her own kombucha and my dad marinated in his conspiracy *du jour*. My middle sister lived in Dubrovnik with a 'musician'/tax accountant, and the older one was an enthusiastic suburbanite in Texas who was deep into her book club and her Instagram account.

We had friction, me and my sisters. I had outright combustion with my parents. But Ray and his brother had a kind of cordial indifference right up until Doug/Dan got sick.

He'd worn out his wife with infidelities, and he was merely a fling for his girlfriends. His parents were dead, and his father's sister wouldn't even let him onto her porch because Doug/Dan had lured her once into a dodgy business venture.

Ray took him in and carried him to doctors. Ray went into debt. Ray tended to his brother as he shriveled and then died.

"I was reading to him when it happened," Ray told me. "*Lord Jim.*"

"Jesus, Ray, he was sick already."

"He was dead a while before I noticed. I was at the part near the end where Jim gets it. Always shakes me up a little. 'I am come in sorrow. I am come ready and unarmed'. I remember waiting for him to breathe, and he just wouldn't."

I knew better than to chime in and try to say something consoling.

"Here's the weird thing," Ray told me in time. "I kept going and finished the book. Just three or four pages, but who'd do that? I was reading to a corpse and knew it."

In a bid to learn from the death of his brother, Ray was trying to be less rigorous, so he quit fooling around with stuff every day about five and sat on his porch, which was starting to feel to me like a brand of shiftlessness. Curtis was still loose, and that Moldovan girl was missing. We had luggage with no people and a PD back to chalking tires, but Ray didn't seem to care, especially after about 4:30, so I was more than a little ready to kick him in the pants when a late-night phone call served for Ray as the jolt he seemed to need.

I laid there half awake hearing just his side of the conversation.

"Whose blood?"

I sat up against the headboard.

"Yeah, twenty minutes." Ray threw back the bedclothes. "Hell, Whit, feed her I guess."

We didn't say much on the way over, had no coffee in us and were barely awake. The cheap replacement phone I'd bought after Curtis had doused my good one beeped twice.

"Farhad?" Ray asked me

I checked my messages. "Yep." I'd been getting texts, six or eight a day, from some guy named Farhad who only had one question for me: "Please can you help me with my studies?"

I'd texted 'yes'. I'd texted 'no'. I'd texted blistering profanity, but Farhad stayed single-minded and unfailingly polite.

Farmer Whit lived in the ass end of nowhere. No street lamps. A lot of patched asphalt. There wasn't a stop sign anywhere out there that hadn't been hit with a shotgun blast.

The porch light was on. I could smell the cattle as soon as I rolled out of Ray's truck, smell the manure anyway along with the tang of pesticide.

Farmer Whit came out in a ratty chambray shirt and a pair of pajama bottoms.

"She's in the shower," he told us.

"She seem all right?" Ray asked him.

Whit shrugged as he held the screen door open and then followed us into the house.

He had bachelor decor, and his place was bachelor neat, which meant stuff was stacked and orderly but nothing was actually clean. As we stood in the front room, Whit whispered to Ray even though the girl they were talking about was down the hall in the bathroom and, from what I'd heard, didn't speak much English at all.

"Shirt's in there with her."

"She injured?"

"Don't think so."

The hinges squeaked as the bathroom door swung open, and I got my first look at Besa once she'd stepped into the hall. She was naked but for a purple bath towel, and she was just holding that in her hand, so we could see old bruises and a couple of new ones, scabby patches particularly up and down her legs.

"I've got a robe somewhere," Whit said and ducked into his bedroom to fetch it.

Ray, for his part, waved at Besa. "Where you been, girl?" he asked her.

She told him quite a lot of something back.

She seemed more giddy than distressed, and when Whit showed up with a bathrobe for her, she flung down her towel and took it but was in no hurry to put it on.

Whit told her something in hayseed Romanian, and she finally slipped into that robe.

"Me and Salvador been boning up," Whit explained. "Just something to do, you know."

"She say anything at all about where she's been?" Ray asked.

"Not yet. Might do it now." Whit spoke to Besa in a strain of Romanian so busted up and wayward that he had to try it twice.

Besa said a full minute's worth of stuff back.

"She was in a car," Whit told us, "and then she was maybe in a house. I'm not sure about the rest of it."

"Where'd she come from tonight?" I asked him.

Whit did what he could by way of putting the question, and Besa gestured and chattered, rattled on for a while.

Whit pointed toward his back door. "Out there somewhere," he said.

I was watching the girl through all this. I call her a girl, but she was past that and ragged, kind of swarthy too like she'd been born into some Moldovan tribe. Regular enough to look at but nothing terribly striking. She was hairy in unfeminine places and had a rangy set of eastern bloc teeth.

"You said blood?" Ray asked Whit, and he went off to the bathroom, came straight back with a man's dress shirt that once had been primarily blue. Not anymore.

It was stained all over. Somebody had gone empty. Ray took the thing in hand and gave it a comprehensive look. This was precisely his sort of business since the longer he hung with it, the stranger it got.

"Your donkey happy now?" I asked him.

"Oh hell yeah," Ray said.

3

Farmer Whit's Mexican buddy rolled in around eight. He'd brought a couple of sausage biscuits for Besa and a fuller vocabulary, mostly Russian but Salvador had worked on his Romanian as well.

"What do we know?" he asked us all while Besa unwrapped a biscuit and shoved the bulk of it into her mouth. I'd heard she had a bottomless appetite and the manners of a coyote, but I'd assumed that was an exaggeration until I saw her eat up close.

Salvador, who had a worldly streak and an internet connection, told me all about life on the ground in the Balanesti Mountains where the natives were keen on shoes and coats but less interested in forks.

The sausage biscuits seemed to make Besa chatty, and Whit and Salvador translated.

"Says they stuck her," Salvador told us, "and she woke up in the trunk."

Besa chewed and swallowed and spoke some more.

"Played sleepy," Whit said. "Guess they didn't stick her good."

"Whose blood on the shirt?" Ray asked.

Salvador put the question to Besa, and she responded with freshet of Russo-Romanian that included what sounded like a name.

"Did she say Blair?"

"Think so," Salvador told me. He checked with Besa and then nodded.

Though it took a while, Salvador and Whit eventually teased out Besa's story. She'd ridden around in a car trunk for longer than she could say and then got put in a building somewhere.

After that, Besa appeared to lose interest. She stood up from the table and crossed to a far cabinet where she came away with a sleeve of saltines. She ripped the wrapper open with her teeth and shoved a stack of crackers into her mouth.

I had a closer look at that bloody dress shirt, which was hanging on a doorknob in Whit's hallway. No holes. Not even a missing button, just a hell of a lot of blood. By the time I stepped back into the kitchen, Besa had curled up on the floor. Whit's mongrel came in from somewhere, all grumpy and adenoidal. The dog curled up against Besa's calves, showed us his underbite, and wheezed.

"Is it the language thing," Ray wanted to know, "or is she just being skimpy with us?"

"Truth is," Whit allowed, "we're probably picking up half of what she says."

"Y'all know any Moldovans?" I asked.

Salvador and Whit let Ray inform me that, yeah, they kind of did.

Ray made me go with him to fetch his Moldovan who, along the way, Ray explained was more of a Russian wetworks guy.

Ray handed me his wallet and had me fish all the folding cash out of it, including the twenty he kept in the secret slot behind his insurance card.

"Ninety-three," I told him.

"That might get him off the boat."

"Boat?" I said and pictured a schooner. Not even close, as it turned out.

The guy lived on a derelict barge a long damn way from the water, cocked up on a mud bank at the end of a swampy trail, and I had to walk up sagging boards to reach the rusty deck.

Ray got nautical for some reason and yodeled out, "Ahoy!" while I stayed busy trying to avoid an open hatchway that gave onto a view of a couple of feet of briny sludge in the hold.

"Define wetworks," I said.

"You know. Sanctioned carnage."

"Who told you that?"

"Guy I know."

"Do we need carnage?"

"Nice to have the option," Ray said. "Better still, he speaks Romanian. Pavel!" Ray shouted the name out twice.

He didn't raise a reply, but we soon enough noticed a large, hairy man looking down at us from up on the cabin roof.

He was shirtless and appeared to be lightly dusted with pulverized rust.

"Pavel, hey."

Pavel lowered his goggles and revealed a couple of pale, unrusted eye sockets.

"Got a minute for us?"

Pavel didn't seem sure.

"Ray Tatum, remember? Brought that Moldovan girl?"

Pavel nodded but only once I'd quit believing he ever would.

"Got a proposition for you."

Pavel stayed where he was and watched us. When he finally spoke, what he said was, "Tea?"

Pavel proved to be quite a specimen up close, had the pelt of an alpaca and the body odor of a possum. Better still, he sounded like a Russian movie villain from 1986.

"So?" Pavel said while the tea was brewing in a big, tarnished samovar.

"Heard about Riga," Ray told him while Pavel buffed three teacups clean with a tube sock. "Bratislava too."

Pavel grunted and then shifted my way. "Lemon," he said. "Cream. No have."

"And that business in Knightsbridge. Guy with the ocelot. That was you as well, I hear."

Pavel chose not to respond but instead poured me a cup of black tea that proved eye-wateringly acidic.

"Sugar?"

"No have."

I noticed he'd cut the toes out of his sneakers and even had ridiculous tufts of hair down there as well.

Pavel pointed at my bruised eye sockets and then jabbed a thumb Ray's way as if to ask me, "He do this?"

I caught myself wondering for a moment what brand of carnage Pavel might get up to, if I just nodded, if I just told him, "Yeah."

This was kind of what chivalry had come to for me, a large, shirtless, filthy Russian inflicting some harm on my behalf in the cabin of a grounded barge. I decided to spare Ray and shook my head.

Pavel grunted and shrugged and then dug enough lint out of his belly button to pack a blunderbuss. When he finally spoke, he said, "Ocelot, yes," and laughed.

"You remember the girl I brought, right?" Ray asked him.

Pavel nodded. "Ruminskiya."

"Her situation's taken kind of a turn," Ray said, and he ran through a few of the details.

Pavel sipped his tea as he heard Ray out. Once it was time for him to say something back, he went with, "Your elbow is close, yet you cannot bite it."

I had to think that was one of those homespun life-on-the-Volga scraps of wisdom, which probably didn't make awfully much sense over there either.

"We need somebody who can protect her," Ray said, "and help her tell us everything she knows. I think you might be the guy."

Pavel nodded like he could see the sense in all that Ray was saying but hardly like he'd decided he'd throw in with us. He finished his tea and considered the leafy dregs in the bottom of his cup. He stirred them with his finger and said in time, "A pig will find mud anywhere."

"Interested?" Ray asked.

"It is possible," Pavel told him. "Tea?" he asked me, but I hadn't found a place to dump my first cup yet.

"Kate might can get you a Bureau contract or something," Ray volunteered to Pavel. I so couldn't that I didn't even bother to give Ray a look.

As it turned out, Pavel was a devoted a freelancer. He tapped his tufted chest and said, "No contract. Money I need for walking around, yes?"

Ray nodded.

"Holiday Inn Express, yes?"

Ray nodded.

"Golden Corral, yes?"

Ray told Pavel, "All right."

Pavel shucked his shorts right in front of us. He was pale and naked beneath, and he put on a pair of long pants that fit him like mom jeans. He fished a Euro-trash shirt out of pasteboard box, sniffed it contemplatively, and then put that on as well. He packed another one just like it in a paper grocery sack with what looked like a pair of bicycle shorts and, I guess, his Dopp kit, which seemed to consist of a half-empty fifth of Smirnoff and a comb.

Pavel pulled the sock he'd cleaned the teacups with onto his left foot and then slipped it back into his toeless sneaker. His right foot went without. As he tied his shoes, he favored us with some additional Russian malarky.

"The fed wolf," he said, "still looks into the forest." Then Pavel carefully rolled shut the neck of his grocery sack and declared, "I am shotgun."

So I rode for two hours in the king cab back seat where the goat had been.

Pavel had to make do with a Hampton Inn, spanking new and smelling of carpet dye. The place was about as close to the highway as you could get without being in traffic, and Pavel confirmed it would satisfy his needs by testing the ground fault outlets in the bathroom.

The nearest Golden Corral was two exits south of the motel, and Pavel insisted on a late lunch before any meaningful work could commence. I'm not a fan of buffets, all those pans heaped with stuff and patrons sidling along to poke and peer at it through the sneeze guard. The whole concept is unappetizing to me, but Pavel was geared just the opposite way and took a kind of childish delight in the wealth of food on offer. He didn't load up on sirloin or chicken but instead carefully piled his plate with modest tastes of nearly everything.

"You Americans," he told us at the table as he moved from yams to slaw to Salisbury steak to custard to cornbread to pasta salad. Then he uncorked some Russian wisdom, if you can call it that.

"The tambourines are good," he said, "when they are behind the mountains."

Ray nodded like he was edified. I poked at my piece of sheet cake.

"Banjos are nice," I told Pavel, "once you've launched them into space."

Pavel laughed and burped and then went off to the bathroom. He returned with his hair slicked back like he'd stuck his head under the tap.

"Again, yes?" And then he hustled off to re-buffet.

By the time we finally got him to the farm, Besa and Whit were on the sofa with Whit's homely dog between them. They were watching a girl make egg foo young on a griddle in a food truck. She sounded Scandinavian and had six or eight pigtails and super-max tattoos.

While Besa and Pavel caught up in Besa's native tongue, me and Ray got the latest on her from Whit, which was mostly dietary.

"How does she eat so much?" Whit wanted to know.

"I've got a nephew like her," Ray told him. "Was like her anyway. Now he's diabetic and fat."

"She will tell all now," Pavel informed us.

"How'd you do that?" Ray asked him.

"All cats," Pavel said, "are gray in the dark."

We all moved into the kitchen, and Pavel and Besa took seats opposite each other at Whit's table. Ray stood next to Pavel and attempted to coach him, would suggest a question that Pavel would quite frequently fail to ask.

Pavel and Besa would indulge in fairly lengthy exchanges, and then Pavel would tell us, "She says 'not exactly'" or "She cannot recall." Which was hardly, to my way of thinking, telling all.

We didn't get much that was concrete or useful for the best part of an hour, and then Besa's glucose level dropped, or something, and she had to eat again. Whit cooked her eggs and onions while me and Ray took Pavel aside and tried to make better sense of everything he'd been hearing.

"So she's got no idea where she's been," Ray asked, "or why she's so important to them?"

"Or even who 'they' are?" I added.

Pavel told us both, "Depozit. You know, warehouse."

"But no location?" I asked him.

"Would seem." Pavel glanced Whit's way. "Tea, yes?"

Whit had an ancient box of Sleepy Time that Pavel openly thought as little of as a man can think of tea. He complained through a mug of it anyway while Besa ate her eggs with her fingers and then sopped her plate with four slices of white bread.

Then Besa told Pavel the Romanian version (I guess) of "All right, let's go," because Pavel returned to his chair and set back into quizzing Besa. He asked her a question that featured the name of the moment, Blair, and Besa responded at lively length while we waited for a translation.

"White man," Pavel told us.

"That his shirt?" Ray asked.

Pavel nodded.

"His blood?" Ray again.

After some Romanian chatter, Pavel told Ray, "Maybe no."

"Whose then?"

Pavel asked, and Besa didn't say exactly but instead gave him a bumpy account of most everything she'd been through, which seemed to largely involve being held in a depozit somewhere.

"There is fight," Pavel told us.

"Who's fighting?" I asked him.

Pavel asked, and Besa responded. "She says . . . men."

"What men?" Ray asked.

Besa spoke further.

"Much stabbing," Pavel told us. "With *otverka*. Screwdriver," he said.

Ray tried again. "What men?"

Pavel spoke some more with Besa who either couldn't say or didn't know.

"They make her sleepy," Pavel told us, "with drugs."

Ray pulled out his phone and did some googling. Once he'd figured a way to filter out the jug-eared, former prime minister, Ray turned up images of a quartet of Mr. Blairs in the vicinity. One of them owned a plumbing supply house. Another had recently celebrated his 98th birthday. The third appeared to be some sort of financial consultant, and the last one was a chiropractor. Ray'd had a bad chiropractic experience, which I'm sure is why he started with him.

He showed Besa a photo of the guy on his phone screen. We could see a part of a patient he was adjusting. "Blair?" Ray asked.

Besa told him a few things back, but the clear thrust of it all was, "No."

The plumbing supply guy got the same response. Besa seemed confused by the geriatric, which left just the financial consultant. Weak chin. Pale complexion. Impeccably parted hair.

Ray handed his phone to Besa, and she became lively in an instant and said quite a lot of heated stuff in her mother tongue. Then she made a show of spitting in the direction of Ray's phone.

Besa stood up, agitated, and shouted all manner of stuff, including something that sounded to me like *om rau*. She all but shrieked it four or five times.

"Bad man," Pavel told us by way of translation. "Devil. Demon from hell. Like that."

4

Ray's phone map took us to an office park out on the bucolic end of Drayton. As office parks go, this one was handsome. Some thought had gone into the campus architecture, and it was more in the way of consistently Georgian than the blocky, usual stuff. The grounds were inviting, lots of paths and shrubby hummocks.

"It's that one." Ray pointed and turned into a lot with a couple of vehicles in it. We climbed out of Ray's truck and headed for the entrance.

The outer door wasn't locked but the receptionist was gone, so we went straight back to the stairwell and up to the second floor. In the corridor, we ran across an East Indian guy in business casual who was eating a pear and playing a game on his phone.

"Mr. Blair?" Ray said and pointed down the hall.

"Yeah," he told Ray and then went responsible. "Hold it. Wait. We're closed. Who are you?"

Ray gave me a glance I could decipher, so I pulled out my credentials and put them right in his face — badge and card — the way you sometimes do.

"Oh," he said. "Yeah. He's spinning. Doesn't like to be interrupted."

"We'll chance it," Ray told him.

We found Mr. Blair riding what looked like a stupidly pricey stationary bike. It was all tubular alloy and Klingon design. Mr. Blair was wearing just shiny red shorts and sneakers some fashion maven had thought too damn hard about.

He was watching the business news on a wall-mounted TV, listening to it through earphones, so I doubt he heard us talking about him as we considered him from the rear.

"If he does so damn much spinning," Ray asked, "why does he look like that?"

He wasn't fat, but he sure was puffy, which went poorly with his weak chin.

"What do you think those shorts are made of?" I asked Ray. They were as shiny as clothing gets.

"The hopes and dreams of orphans," he told me just as Mr. Blair got a feeling and glanced back our way.

He didn't talk to us at first but jerked out his earbuds and called to his colleague, "Mason!"

The East Indian guy rushed up at a trot. "They're FBI," he said.

Mr. Blair dismounted, snatched a towel off his handlebars. He swabbed himself and didn't at all seem to mind that we were watching. Like the vast run of dumpy white guys, he'd decided he was a catch.

He huffed and wiped. "Knackered anyway," he announced. He motioned with his fingers to get a look at my badge and card. I handed them over. He motioned for Ray's, but Ray just shook his head.

"Your name has come up in an inquiry," I told him.

"Who's he?"

"My associate," I said.

Ray pulled out his phone, brought a photo of Besa onto the screen and showed it to Mr. Blair. "Do you know this woman?" Ray asked him.

"What sort of associate?"

"ICE," I said. "Undercover."

Mr. Blair had a good long look at Ray. The sweat-stained shirt, the jeans, the boots. "No," he said presently. "I don't know that woman."

"Might want to be sure on this," I told him.

He looked again. "She could be one of our cleaning girls. Mason!"

Mason came back in, had a look at the photo and told us he'd never seen her before. Him I believed.

"I can give you the number of the service we use." Mr. Blair had another glance at Ray's phone screen. "Might be one of theirs."

He led us into the corridor and down to his office where he went straight to the wet bar and got himself a water from his puny fridge and then plucked a t-shirt off his desk and finally covered his flabby self up.

"What did she do?" he asked us.

I ignored him. "So you're an investment counselor?"

He nodded.

"Could she be a customer?" I asked him.

"That the only picture you've got?" he asked Ray.

In fact, Ray had several more, including one of Besa eating, shoveling in what looked like pot roast with only her crooked fingers. Mr. Blair lingered over that one, even shifted it around like he couldn't quite understand which side was up.

"If you're here," he said to Ray, "it must be some immigration thing. Aside from Mason, all our people are USDA prime. And Mason's working on it. Marrying a local girl."

Mr. Blair seemed awfully relaxed for a man getting visited by a pair (as far as he knew) of federal agents. People usually go squirrelly, even the squeaky clean ones.

He drained his entire bottle of water while Ray set out on a tour of his office to have a leisurely look at the knickknacks and the photos on the walls. From where I was standing, I could see mostly white guys on what looked like team-building jaunts.

Those pictures interested Ray enough that he raised his phone and took a few snaps until Mr. Blair noticed and objected. "Whoa now," he said and then turned to me. "You've got no warrant, and that bloke doesn't even have a badge."

Ray pocketed his phone and came back over to join us.

"Anything else?" Blair asked. "I've got somewhere to be."

"Ok if we come back tomorrow, talk a little more?"

Mr. Blair had a business card for me, and he knew just where to find it. Reston, Jones & Abernathy, attorneys in D.C..

"Talk to them," he said, winked even. "They'll talk to me."

Ray put down his tailgate, and we sat on it for a bit out in the office park lot.

"What was that accent?" Ray asked. "Knackered? Bloke?"

"Sounded like Madonna British."

If I'd still been smoking, I would have been on my third cigarette by then. I knew from past experience, Ray needed to make his gradual way to something pertinent. While he hardly looked busy, he was actually cogitating at full speed.

"Say you've got some girls," Ray finally said as he picked bark off a stick, "and one keeps making trouble. You've brought them here for whoring or something, and one just won't stick to the plan."

"Think she's special to them?" I asked.

"You've been around her. She seem special?"

"Eats for twelve."

"And Whit says she mops a rug real nice, but if it was you and me who shipped her in from Moldova, how fed up with her would we be by now?"

More cogitation followed, more stick peeling. Ray shushed me and made me listen to evening birdsong for longer than I would have liked, long enough for Ray to finally arrive at the nugget of his trouble.

"We're a long way into this thing," he told me, "to not know more than this."

"I had one of these maybe five years ago," I said. "Killeen, Texas. I told you about it. Remember?"

Ray didn't and shook his head.

We thought some guy was stealing cigarettes, but it wasn't quite that simple. The smokes were usually off-brand stuff, the cheap ones they sell out of reservations. They sent me down when the agent who usually covered Killeen got sick.

A semi got jacked from a parking lot at an I-35 truck stop. The driver was taking a shower and came out to a big empty spot. He didn't care much about the truck or the load, but his dog had been in the cab. Kelso, a geriatric terrier with a bad hip and a poor attitude. The cigarettes ended up in Nevada. The dog, in Portland, Maine.

"Excuse me," Ray said.

"Yeah, Maine."

"You never told me this. Alive and well?"

I nodded. "He wandered into some kind of hippie market. They got him scanned. He had a chip."

"Happy reunion?"

"Very. Then it happened all over again."

"Killeen to Maine?"

I shook my head. "Mankato, Minnesota."

"Kelso?"

I nodded. "Somebody found him in a park."

"Driver's got to be in on it."

"That's what I was thinking."

The driver had two exes and a flock of casual girlfriends, enough to seem like an overabundance for a man with his limited charms. I suspected he was slippery enough to be getting paid to be scarce and accommodating, and the stuff with the dog was so he could come off seeming victimized.

"I'd have been right there with you," Ray told me.

"Everybody was," I said, "but the exes and the girlfriends all checked out, and if the driver was getting paid, he certainly hid the money well.

Ray took a stab. "One of the ex's boyfriends or maybe some shiftless in-law. Feels like half thievery, half messing with the guy."

"I thought of all that, but . . ." I shook my head.

Ray gestured for me to continue.

"Third time in, we caught a break. A trooper stopped the truck on 40. Tucumcari, New Mexico. Boy at the wheel was Navajo. Sixteen years old. Didn't even have a license for a car. And it was just him alone. No dog."

"Kid spill the beans?"

I shook my head. "Worse even than Moldovan. He was a minor, and he was completely mute."

"Like . . . teenage mute, or . . .?

"Couldn't talk. Never had."

"Write?"

"Wouldn't."

"Kind of a problem."

"It gets better. The dog shows up in Pensacola."

"You're just fucking with me, aren't you?"

I shook my head. "Our agent in Texas recovered. I got sent back to D.C.. The case was still open last time I bothered to check."

"What the hell kind of story's that?"

"The kind that's not about a dog."

I let Ray get to it in his own time because I knew he would. He finally asked the evening air, "What kind of story's this?"

Blair

1

I can smell it. The feral wallowing. The mongrel urges. The gypsy conniving and shiftless deceit. The grim and creeping woggishness of it all. That's what I tell the lads anyway because they come to us hungry for guidance, equipped with fury that needs a nudge, a channel where it can flow. I coach and consult. Organize and aim. Break and corral when I need to. Just raging around won't take you far. The skill is all in the control.

We started casually as a kind of club — on the links, on the courts, in the lounges — and we were four for a pretty fair while until we found an apostate among us and decided, for purity's sake, to be just three.

Kyle and I had been roommates once. He turned out to be part Turk on his mother's side and so had a touch of dusky blood and probably a turban or two in the woodpile. That alone wouldn't have been disqualifying. I like a reclamation project, but Kyle was also carting around a strain of ethical arrogance.

He believed he had moral standards the rest of us fell short of. Kyle never came right out and said as much, but I knew him well enough to tell, and I found I wasn't equipped to tolerate high-handedness from his sort.

Kyle showed us his colors during an incident at the club. It was the four of us together, and we were on fifteen that doglegs right. Geoffrey is a serial shanker and yanked his drive into the woods. We all went in to have a look because Geoffrey's balls are stupid expensive, and he has a pout every time one gets away.

There's a pond just through the woods on fifteen, and a boy was fishing there. He was sitting on an upturned bucket like they do, holding an honest-to-God cane pole, smoking a Cool (of course).

Douglas, because he's a lawyer and can't begin to help it, explained to that boy he was on private property and had no right to fish.

Geoffrey, who's a lot less expansive than Douglas, simply told him, "Go the hell on."

He was probably still mad about the shank. He'd paid the pro good money to cure it, and he raised his driver like braining a colored boy was a thing he could make that golf club do.

That boy took a puff on his cigarette and told Geoffrey something low and sullen back. He seemed to know instinctively that Geoffrey was all mouth and no trousers. They've got a talent for it, the lot of them, and they usually slag off the ones they can.

"You believe this?" Geoffrey asked us like Geoffrey always does once he's gotten called out for being a blowhard, for being (at bottom) Geoffrey.

That boy started winding his line around his pole, wouldn't look at us at all, and seemed to think it would do if he took his gear and his bucket and went home. That's kind of the trouble generally in this world, no regard for consequences. People get up to wretched stuff and shrug it off when they're called out.

There was a time for me when evicting that boy from the course would have been sufficient, but I've come to believe that sort of response is grievously incomplete. So when he tried to step away from the bank, I showed him the business end of my four iron.

"Not today," I told him and pointed directly across the pond.

He did some mumbling, like they do, and then tried to come up again, but I was settled in my mind about how things would go and caught him flush in the gut. His wind left him, and he staggered a step or two.

"That way," I said and pointed across the pond.

He looked ready for a squabble until Douglas and Geoffrey raised their clubs as well.

Kyle had brought a ball retriever into the woods, a flimsy, telescoping thing, but I doubt he would have acted differently if he'd been armed with a chainsaw.

"Go," I told that boy and pointed again.

Geoffrey and Douglas made threatening noises and menaced him from my flanks. Kyle didn't do a blessed thing.

That still wasn't enough to hurry him. He muttered and mumbled, waded in up to his knees and stopped to glance back and grumble some more.

He looked pretty unhappy as he waded out, which was just what I was after. Then the bottom fell away, and I got more from that boy than I would have dared to dream. He couldn't swim, and the fear of nothing solid beneath took hold of him hard, especially once his bucket filled with water and sank.

He flopped around and let go of his pole, glared our way but couldn't bring himself to call to us for help. There wasn't anything dignified about him, just ongoing insolence, and he made a bid to reach the far bank but lacked the skill and the buoyancy for it. He ended up staying in essentially one place and beating the water instead.

"He's in trouble."

Those were the first words Kyle had bothered to say. The whole time we'd been tangling with that boy Kyle stood apart and added nothing. Only once we had him right where we wanted did Kyle find an objection to raise.

Dougie and Geoffrey laughed. Kyle took off a shoe.

The boy managed somehow to work himself sideways and into a scrubby bush hanging over the edge of the pond. He had plenty to say to us as he climbed out of the water, but it was just the usual muttered trash we couldn't begin to understand.

We finished our round at twilight and had our Mount Gay and bitters in the grill. Me and Douglas and Geoffrey did anyway, but Kyle claimed to have a commitment.

"Dinner thing," he said, but he was lying. I could always tell with him. We weren't his kind of people anymore.

I felt sure by then Kyle needed a serious dose of retraining, so we organized a meeting out at Geoffrey's dad's place. The old man calls it a hunting camp, but it's just a couple of hundred acres of raw land and a trailer. There's boggy ground on the north end, and that's where we ended up. I told Kyle we were inducting fresh recruits into our brigade, an activity that had gotten commonplace for us since there are lots of lads around hungry for affirmation, looking for brothers who hate the way they hate.

We usually have a bonfire when we're swearing those boys in, and I could tell Kyle was looking for flames and smoke as we dropped off of the hillside onto soupy ground. Kyle had stopped and was turning my way when I shoved him onto the ground. Geoffrey and Douglas both kicked him after I'd suggested they ought to, and then I pulled out my .380 and pressed the barrel to his neck.

I'd prepared what I meant to say to Kyle about loyalty and purpose. It was all intended to be a tough love sort of thing, and I'd only just started when he lurched and bucked, knocked into me so hard as to cause me to squeeze the trigger and fire off a round.

The bullet went in below his ear, and Kyle flattened out and groaned. He wasn't dead. It's possible that he wasn't even dying, but Kyle had suddenly made himself into something we wouldn't want to explain, so I took actual aim and fired again.

Douglas and Geoffrey were surprised, of course, and stood there merely gawking. I could tell they needed a word from me, so I supplied it.

"Dig."

~~~

I carry a picture of Patricia to keep me alert to the wages of treachery. She came in as a temp, and we kept her on. I kept her on, if I'm honest, because Patricia was somehow simultaneously bubbly and wry. Almost chirpy but also sardonic. You don't see that blended much. She was lanky, mostly legs, and usually wore her hair up in a way that came off as thrown together and yet engineered to be beguiling.

I never let her near my lad stuff, thought I could do that at the time, hold parts of myself in quarantine and closed off from each other. But then I met Patricia's mother who introduced me to her boyfriend, and he turned out to be some kind of Pacific island half breed. I couldn't help, of course, but wonder what Patricia's father had been like.

I said enough hard stuff to Patricia about her family to make things chilly between us, and eventually I did actually hit her but only with my open hand. Yes, it was late, and I'd shown up at her house. Yes, she was seeing somebody else by then, but I'd convinced myself that we'd not yet worked through all our issues.

Her new boyfriend came to my office the following day. He marched straight in past Mason and shut and locked my office door.

"Who are you?" What else could I say?

He snorted. "You fucking know."

I did, of course, on account of the surveillance, but I wouldn't give him the satisfaction.

He was a big guy, and I did my best to help him get the spunk out of his system. He jerked me around and punched me some, but I don't rise to that sort of bait.

Mason brought me a damp towel. "Stitches maybe," he said once he'd looked me over, but his people are from Peshawar, so what in the hell would Mason know?

We were testing the starch of a fresh batch of lads, and I put three of them on the boyfriend. They laid for him in the lot outside the homewares store where they beat him with their fists and then beat him with the garden spade he'd bought before civilians interceded they way they far too often will.

One of the lads even got arrested. It was his car they were driving, but he did his bit in county and never said a word. That's more than I would have gotten from Kyle, maybe even from Geoffrey and Douglas, and I took that lad on as my right hand once the law had turned him loose.

Everybody called him Kip, and he'd been knocking around after three tours as a Marine. Once I got to know him better and saw the harm the man could do, I had to wonder how Patricia's boyfriend even survived. Sure the guy had come away with a limp and a plate, but it could have been far worse.

After Patricia, I moved on from regular women and started hiring a girl instead. She had a broker named Steve. You could only reach him through a referral. Mine came from Douglas' uncle. He's sixty-something and in banking with grown children and a dead wife and no interest in romance. Not the kind anyway you have to cast around for, labor at and cultivate, but he's happy enough to purchase it whenever he gets an itch.

I met him for a drink one evening to feel him out about a loan, and a half hour in, a woman showed up and joined us at the bar. She was forty maybe and lovely but in an understated way. Expensive clothes. Tall and thin. He introduced her as Barbara.

I asked Doug about her the next day.

"Bought and paid for," Douglas explained.

I let my interest be known, and in a week or so got an office visit from Steve. He'd scheduled a regular appointment for a consultation, had left Mason with the impression he had an inheritance to invest, but once Mason had shown him in, Steve said, "I understand you're Haywood's friend."

Things snapped into focus for me. "You're that Steve."

He nodded. "Is there a Mrs. Blair? Hardly verboten, but we like to know."

I shook my head. He gave me a price.

"Is that for Barbara?"

"If you like, but we have other options."

Four as it turned out, but two of them were too exotic to suit. One was a ginger (not my thing), but the last one had potential. Steve showed me a photo of her hiking in the sort of skimpy clothes you'd wear to hike in if you pulled down a couple of grand a night.

"Shelly," he told me. "Five eight, one twenty-five."

"She American?"

"Hundred percent. Like 'em midwestern?"

I didn't much and shook my head.

"Good. California girl. Raised by vegans. No bad habits ever."

"How do I meet her?"

"Easy," Steve said. "We set up an account."

Nothing is seedy anymore. Everything has gotten so antiseptic and efficient, so very click-to-order and space-aged that almost anything you get up to feels about like everything else. I used my Facebook login to set up my account with Steve and tied it to the company Amex card. It all took about five minutes.

Together we made an appointment for me to meet Shelly for coffee at the place inside the bookstore down near the Dollar Tree.

"Norman?" She said it just the way my mother used to. She was wearing what looked to be tennis togs and was carrying a bag with a paperback in it, a travel book by Evelyn Waugh.

I'd say we hit it off, but our connection was never in doubt, or existed primarily in the form of a charge against my corporate card. We talked about me almost entirely, and some of it was even true. Then we talked about her a little, and I doubted everything she said, but she was lithe and agreeable and entirely mine for as long as I could afford her. Then she'd conveniently disappear until I could afford her again.

After Patricia, that sort of thing struck me as useful and refreshing because, with regular girls, they can be right in your arms and faithless all at once. Thinking of where they'd rather be, dreaming about who with and how, but with Shelly the devotion was built into the price. The clothes too and the conversation. Sullen and distant weren't allowed. Not by her anyway, but I could be a knob whenever I wanted, and Shelly was sure to keep on being cordial and understanding back.

She was close to perfect, this girl, and pricey enough to need to be.

I got together with Douglas' uncle one day for lunch to pick his brain. By then Shelly and I had moved well beyond coffee, and she'd stayed over a couple of nights. I couldn't decide how far to take things with her. What topics might be off-limits or if we should talk beyond piffle at all.

"They do all sorts of digging," Doug's uncle told me. "It's good business for Steve to find out who you are."

There was some dodgy stuff to dig up about me if you knew just where to look. Not criminal necessarily, but I've long held some *outrè* opinions, and I've sure aired out my philosophy at various spots on the web. Not that I've ever been ashamed of anything I've thought, but there were people I needed in business who wouldn't much like the stuff at my core.

"Ever told yours anything private? Secret? Ever really confided in her?" I asked.

"Maybe, once or twice," Douglas' uncle allowed. "I just don't have much to tell. Might be different with you."

He laughed, so I laughed too.

I knew from Douglas that his uncle had a thing for women's feet and, given a chance, would shove a toe in a spot that was best not contemplated, and I imagine he thought I had something like that to clue in my girl about.

Mine was worse. I hated people I didn't even know, wanted them dead and punished, would have preferred them incinerated. That's not the sort of thing you can just up and tell a girl, even one who's taking money to tolerate your kinks and quirks. Somehow, though, for the sake of my integrity, I felt like I had to come at least a little clean with Shelly. Honesty lite is how I thought of it, and I started by running down a couple of Pacific rim races and then went after Africans one evening in a pretty unsavory way.

Shelly didn't care. She'd had a black roommate who stole her stash of pills, and Shelly allowed she would have torn her to pieces if she'd only known how to fight.

"I might can help you with that," I told her. "I happen to know a Marine."

And that's how I came to put her with Kip, which led to a pile of trouble.

2

Shelly proved to be a schemer, though I was a long time catching on. Probably because we had a transactional thing and I was paying for her affections, which left me doubtful she'd get up to any business she couldn't bill. But then she started badgering me about a gentleman named Clifford, an old buddy of hers with Eastern bloc connections she wanted to hook me up with.

"He'll get us girls," Shelly told me. "The kind that are up for anything. Don't tell me your lads couldn't do with some of that."

I wasn't sure what my lads could do with. They hardly seemed a romantic bunch, but Shelly was so insistent that I took a meeting with this Clifford at a diner up by Manassas in a blighted shopping plaza. Their specialty was a spaghetti omelet — eggs, pasta, meat sauce, cheese — that looked pre-digested on the plate.

Shelly and Clifford had kind of a jolly reunion once they'd clapped eyes on each other, and when they hugged, I couldn't help but notice Clifford's hand on Shelly's ass. She gave him a loud, moist kiss on the cheek and seemed a touch over-delighted to see him.

I'd say Clifford was near sixty and trying to pass for forty-five. He'd colored his hair and appeared to have done something drastic to his teeth. Too white and so big that his lips didn't fit so awfully well around them. I'm pretty sure he was wearing some kind of corset, probably five-hundred-dollar shoes, and a gold watch you could have served a sandwich on.

"Norman." He finally turned my way. "Pleasure." I got a dose of sandalwood cologne.

Shelly explained to me who Clifford was and explained to Clifford about me, just cursory stuff. We both knew what we were there for.

"How many?" he asked.

Shelly said to me, "Let's do eight."

"Slow down. Where are they from?" I asked Clifford, "and how would you get them to me?"

"All over and my problem." He had a look at his nails and did some cuticle maintenance.

"Do they know what they're getting into? What I'm buying?" I don't like confusion and duplicity as a rule. 'Say what you mean and do what you need' is rather a motto with me.

Clifford responded with his version of the wants and illusions of economic refugees. "They tell us what they're hoping for, and we say that's what they're getting."

"Use them for whatever, right?" Shelly chimed in.

Clifford shrugged. He certainly didn't care, and he let me know, because of Shelly, I was in line for one of his special rates.

I watched as Clifford wrote a number on his placemat. "That's for eight," he told me. He knocked two hundred off when I tried to dicker him down and then stood up like he'd walk away until I said, "All right."

Those foreign girls were paying him to come. I'd be paying him to let them, so Clifford must have been making out just fine.

"You'll pick them up at BWI," he told me. "I'll give you plenty of notice."

And that's how it happened. I'd gone up there meaning to settle nothing, was only taking the meeting because Shelly wanted me to, but I came out of that diner a flesh merchant, I guess.

I suspected we'd need to corral those girls at first, like strange dogs you've brought home from the pound, so I had Douglas find us a spot with a barn or a shed that would likely serve. That wasn't much of a challenge for him since property was going begging all over, and he put a crew of lads onto building some kind of cage.

I organize and delegate, am most effective that way, and once Douglas had sent me photos of the work his crew was doing, I hunted up Shelly to tell her all about it since those eight girls were her idea. I located her out at the farm where Kip was training up recruits, the place where she'd been taking regular self-defense lessons from him, and the two of them gave me a demonstration with knives in what passed for a yard. There was a trio of lads around, some rusty junk, a filthy goat.

Two of the lads knew well enough to address me only as gaffer, but the third young man forgot himself and said, "Hello, Mr. Blair."

"Pardon?" I gave him a chance to make a correction. It wasn't my habit to pick at the lads, but if I had a firm rule, it was 'no names, no how'. Only Sir or only Gaffer.

"Hi," he told me and said one time more, "Mr. Blair."

Shelly and Kip were in the middle of some knifey choreography, but Kip was sufficiently tuned in to hear what was going on and so broke off from Shelly and stalked right over to throw that boy to the ground.

"Who's he?" Kip asked the lad, had a foot on his throat by then.

The lad said, "Oh. Right. Gaffer. I forgot."

That was good enough. I could be gracious. I gave the boy a hand up.

His name was Curtis, and he was Kip's gopher and more than a little proud about it. I let him stand with me while Kip and Shelly put on a kind of show. Shelly had picked up moves and lethal techniques and showed some of them off. She'd pull up just short of puncturing Kip and then name the artery she was barely avoiding.

Kip gave me a tour of the bunkhouse, a smelly sty where some old coot had died and had laid around for a while. The place stank of cheap, sweet pipe tobacco and overheated Crisco, and Kip and his charges hadn't troubled themselves to straighten it up awfully much.

I didn't say anything about the mess, didn't want to be a nagging gaffer, and instead I talked to Kip about the girls who were coming in.

"The lads are primed," he told me. "And I'd say touched and grateful, you know? Nobody's ever done much for them. Ever bought them shit."

"Tell them the gaffer says to make those girls last."

"I'll do it," Kip assured me. "They probably won't."

Our cargo arrived on a Tuesday night. Clifford was there to meet the group as they filtered out of customs. We'd left the recruiting entirely up to him, so I can't say what those ladies had been promised or where they thought they'd be heading from the airport and why.

Kip was my eyes and ears up there, was driving the van we'd rented, and I'm told Clifford kept those girls calm with a lot of soothing patter, and all of them loaded up with Kip except for one with qualms. Something didn't seem quite right to her, and she rattled on about it, buttonholed Clifford to quiz him and just wouldn't get in the van.

Clifford had committed to memory rote phrases of various Black Sea mongrel languages, but he lacked what he needed to respond to the woman in any worthwhile way, so instead he pulled out an auto-injector. It seems he carried a couple at all times. Ketamine and propofol were Clifford's narcotics of choice, and whenever he couldn't talk his way out of some combustible upset, Clifford would fish out an injector and try anesthesia instead.

He rolled the bothersome woman into the boot of his sedan while Kip pulled out of the airport with his load.

Aside from that, I'm told things went as smoothly as they could, even once Kip had reached that farm where our lads had built a cage. The plan was the girls would go right in and have a day or two to settle, but some lads immediately took against the one who looked like a gypsy, and they started debating ways to punish her that turned into a fight.

I heard from Kip there was a regular melee and grievous harm was inflicted on some lads.

"Cut up pretty bad. Kind of doubt they'll mend. We did what we could, but . . ." He shrugged.

"And the girls?" I asked.

Kip told me, "Fine, all but the gypsy and maybe the one that had a go at Clifford."

It turned out Clifford had driven her to the goat farm where she'd popped out of his trunk and bit him hard, so Clifford had smacked her around and had paid a few lads to shut her up in a cellar.

"My property," I reminded Kip. "Tell Clifford to let it go."

Kip was about to do just that when Shelly stepped in and kept him from it. The way Kip told it, they were in the bunkhouse kitchen, him and Shelly and Clifford.

"We were just standing there talking," Kip informed me. "Or him and Shelly were talking anyway, and she asked him if he remembered some night they'd spent together at the Greenbrier, and it sound like he'd tossed her around and kicked her something. I don't know exactly what, but I guess Shelly had been kind of sitting on it ever since."

According to Kip, she pulled out her KA-BAR and touched Clifford with it twice.

"Nothing but artery. Dead on target. Spray went everywhere."

"So that's why I got to meet Clifford?"

Kip couldn't say. "We just picked up and left. Too big a mess to clean."

I asked him, "What about the girl, the one in the cellar?"

"Got loose or something, I hear."

~~~

I am firmly devoted to the virtue of keeping things simple in this life, and I couldn't help but lay the gory Shelly and Clifford disaster against the tidy job I'd made of sweet Amanda back in the day.

We went to college together, and Amanda had stepped in as my backup girlfriend when Cheryl, the girl I preferred, threw herself at a boy in my botany class whose deepest personal asset was the dimple in his chin.

So I opted instead for Amanda who was a Presbyterian and optimistic about life for no rational reason at all. She was pretty like a girl who could have maybe won a pageant as a child, but she'd made some poor hair choices since and hadn't shed her baby fat. I'd danced with her once at a big campus do but only because Cheryl was taken, and it was a slow dance so I'd groped her a bit. This was college after all.

Amanda had decided my pawing was meaningful, convinced herself we had a connection, and I let her think she was right. She wasn't nearly enough of a Presbyterian to be chaste and wholesome, and I needed the sort of outlet Cheryl wouldn't let me have.

We were an appalling match, thrown together by proximity and convenience, and I intended to walk away from her, but I knew she'd come apart, and I'd have to comfort her for probably a month and make noises like I wanted her for a friend. I had papers to write and exams to take, and I had my eye on a brunette by then.

She had an iron cross neck tattoo and rolled her own Navy Cut smokes, and this was well back before even your wrinkled grandmother had a dolphin inked onto her ankle. This girl was exotic and angry, seemed delightfully incensed about half the time.

So Amanda and I were finished, and I took her out canoeing to tell her. I'd decided it'd be best to confine her in a boat so she'd be right there where she'd have to hear me, couldn't go all jolly and frantic and launder my clothes or hoover the rug.

We were on a lake, had it all to ourselves, and once we were well out away from the shore where Amanda could pitch a fuss and go unnoticed, I told her everything I'd decided to say. I was decent back then and borderline thoughtful, so I didn't try to devastate her but just cataloged our differences and made clear to Amanda where I stood.

She started shaking and said some blubbery stuff I could hardly understand. Then she leaned over backward and pitched out of the boat. It was March, and Amanda wasn't just fully dressed but had on a topcoat and a pair of boots. Like me, she'd been sitting on her life preserver, and when she popped up and sucked air, she cried out, "Norman, help me. Please!"

I do believe I intended to, but once she'd grabbed the blade of my paddle, instead of drawing her up and out of the water, I pushed her under and down.

I did it gingerly at first, experimentally, and I remember wondering what exactly I was up to. Amanda knew sooner than

I did. I could see it in her eyes, that look that said, "You're the beast I feared you'd be."

I had a glance around. There was no one to see us, and holding her under wasn't much of a chore since she kind of wanted to sink anyway.

She went blue and then sort of a ghastly white as I drifted around and watched her. Once she was gone for certain, I jumped in as well and dragged her to shore because that seemed like the sort of thing a caring human would do.

When it came time to explain what had happened, I merely left out the pushing and then drove myself home while I ate the chips and the sandwiches Amanda had packed. What in this world could be tidier than that?

Douglas knew a deputy a little, some meathead from his gym, and Dougie ended up giving the man some juice for the information we needed and then swung by my office to pass along the news.

"Whitley Romer," he told me. "5240 Old Highway Six."

"Sure it's our girl?"

Douglas nodded. "Sounds like she's move in."

"Country people," I said, "and their stinking hospitality."

I gave the task to Kip and Shelly, left all of it up to them. Just supplied them with the address and sent them on, had no clue what they'd get up to until afterward when they called me from the old mattress ticking plant. They had her. She was doped up with one of Clifford's injectors, and they wanted input from me on how I thought it best to proceed.

Now that the girl had been enough of a hairball to earn the gaffer's attention, I felt like I ought to drive out and maybe deal with her myself.

That old plant had been shut down for decades and was located away from everything on the bank of a dried up creek. There were a couple of tall, red-brick smokestacks and a trio of long, low red-brick buildings. No unbroken glass anywhere and weeds in every spot they could grow. Somebody had thrown up a fence around the property and then had left it to stand neglected, so the gates were all off their hinges and whole sections had rusted and failed.

They had the girl on the gritty cement floor, lying there in only her panties.

"We sure this is her?" I turned her over with my foot. She was a lumpy, hairy thing for a girl.

"It's her." Kip's boy Curtis was talking to me. Then he added, "Mr. Blair."

I felt like I'd given him all the chances a he rated, and I lost the plot there for maybe half a minute, waved the boy over to me, pulled the screwdriver out of his pocket and stuck him with it a fair few times. Up his front and down his back, had to hold him up near the end so I could say, "Gaffer," into his ear.

Shelly eased over once I'd finished and helped me out of my bloody shirt. I remember she took time to nibble an earlobe and tell me, "Clever boy."

3

I was half expecting somebody but hardly the two who came. A battered field agent and her low-life buddy who smelled like he'd been sleeping in his truck.

It was a simple matter to deflect and parry them since they'd arrived knowing nothing at all. My chore as they quizzed me was to keep a firm lid on exactly how nettled I was.

Did I know the girl? She sure seemed to know me. They had phone pics of the creature, her hair a mass of tangles, her mouth half full of food.

I gave those photos my full attention like a decent citizen might. Those two were obviously fishing, asking whatever popped into their heads. They seemed to hope I'd grow uneasy and start to fill their gaps and lulls. I don't know who they thought they were talking to, why they imagined that might work.

I had a suite of offices, a thriving investment business, a credenza with chummy photographs on it. I was riding a three thousand dollar stationary bike when they found me and wearing sneakers you have to know somebody to buy. Every visible thing about me contradicted why they'd come, so all I needed to do was look stymied by their questions and bewildered by the peculiar turn my evening had taken.

There was no need to cobble up decent answers. I just had to not know a girl I didn't actually know, which left me free to study the pair of them, and they were almost certainly a pair. I could tell by the way they deferred to each other, no signaling required.

They ended up hanging around in the parking lot for a little while. I went into the darkened office next to mine and watched them perch and talk. They were sitting on a pickup tailgate and chewing (I decided) on their meager details, and the longer they stayed, the more irritated I got.

That's mostly why I hit her. I'd never done it before, so I learned that night how much my Shelly actually liked a punch.

Her nose bled fairly luxuriously, on a pillowcase, on the top sheet. "I've been awful," Shelly said as she curled my fingers into a fist. "And you can't blame Kip. It's all my fault we let the girl get away."

They gotten too busy disposing of Curtis, hadn't kept things simple and tidy, so what could I possibly do but punch her again, and again, and again.

Steve, the glorified pimp and manager, demanded a sit down once he'd seen her. We met in the parking lot of a Sheetz where I climbed into Steve's Land Rover and endured a lecture from him on the protocols and economics of the high-end escort business, which all ended in a fee for damages he wrote on his palm.

I had a glance and told him, "Don't think so."

"Oh?"

"She likes it. Wants it."

"Not on my dime."He pointed at his hand.

I shook my head. "Hard pass."

Steve grumbled and shifted and got as far as, "Look," before I cut him off.

"No more money from me," I told him. It's not like that anymore."

I waved. My boys had been waiting for it, and three lads climbed onto Steve's backseat. Steve glanced at them. Looked at me.

"I have some of them," he said, "but mine are bigger. Blacker. Meaner."

"Yeah, well, yours aren't here."

I grabbed a healthy handful of Steve's hair — the bit in the back that wasn't plugs or weave or whatever he had going on up top — and I slammed him hard against the steering wheel, which served to set off the lads who visited on Steve a bit of a drubbing.

"High-strung, these lads," I explained.

Steve made a noise.

"Forget Shelly," I told him.

We all got out. Steve made a noise again.

I thought Shelly would be safe enough, decided Steve wouldn't spoil a commodity, but there seemed a fair chance he'd turn his larger, black thugs loose on me. Accordingly, I consulted with Kip and the lads, and we settled on plans and precautions, which proved unnecessary once Shelly had called and said to me, "Come home."

Steve's Land Rover was parked in my driveway, and Shelly came out of the house when I rolled up.

She opened the tailgate and revealed a lumpy something underneath what looked like my bedspread.

"I told him to leave.  Said I'd cut him."

She lifted a corner of the spread to show me a lacerated bit of Steve.  We appeared to be an awfully long way from Evelyn Waugh.

Rowdy

1

I left a whole boot in it. That's how deep it was. Walked right out of the damn thing, and it took two of us to pull it lose.

You couldn't drive anywhere near the place but had to park at a trailer up by a spring head and walk along the spine of the ridge and then down into a boggy patch that covered the best part of an acre. It was all soupy black ground, rotted mulch gone to dirt.

I had rubber boots somewhere, thought they were in the prowler but ended up tromping on down in my ropers, the good pair I'd just cleaned and waxed.

Only two of the corpse crew had found the place yet, and neither one of them was the chief diddler but just the boy with the glasses who wouldn't ever look at you straight and big Debbie or Donna or something with the mustache. They were standing and gawking like everybody else.

The guy who'd found him was across the way talking to Keith and them, and since I wasn't about to wade through more muck, I sent Gwen over to fetch him. He was one of those Trueloves who hunts any damn where whenever he feels the need, and he came wading my way, had the gear for it — boots up past his knees.

Sheriff," he said. "Hell of a thing."

"What are you even doing back in here?"

He shrugged.

They didn't yet have him uncovered altogether because it was just Debbie/Donna and the boy with the glasses fiddling around with garden trowels. The black, boggy water flowed back in wherever the dirt came out.

He didn't look fresh, but it seemed like the muck had largely kept him from rotting, so his skin was loose and greasy and he was an awfully ghoulish sight, not the sort of thing I'd want to run across in the woods.

That Truelove, for his part, didn't appear much affected. He dug out a plug of chaw and shoved it in his mouth.

"I'm going to get you to write it up," I told him.

He groaned like I'd asked him to rotate my tires once he'd painted my house.

By then I had to move somewhere else or sink on out of sight, so I clomped on over to have a closer look at the body.

"Shot," Debbie/Donna informed me. "Two times in the head." She parted the victim's lips with a stick to show me his shattered teeth.

He was wearing what we used to call a car coat, the pricey kind with bone buttons shaped like little tusks and one of those sweaters with a rolled neck like you see in catalogs.

The boy with glasses found a wallet and the dead man's driver's license. "Richard Kyle Everly," he told me, but I'd already suspected as much.

His wife and his father-in-law had been all over us since Mr. Everly had failed to come home a while back. Daddy-in-law was some kind of lawyer and so operated by default at around Defcon two. I don't think I'd known him for an hour before he was threatening to have my job.

We'd located Richard Kyle Everly's car in a mini-mall parking lot, and we'd learned from one of his lady colleagues that they'd had kind of a thing.

"Didn't last," she told us. "Kyle believed . . . funny stuff." We could never quite pin her down on funny how exactly. It just sounded like he was a harder man than she'd hoped he'd be. Hard enough, as it turned out, to get shot in the woods.

We were still waiting for forensics when I showed Ray and FBI the Everly file.

"Anything in his car?" Ray wanted to know.

"Coffee mug. CDs. Chapstick. Like that."

"Any reason to think he was meeting somebody?"

I couldn't say. Didn't know.

Ray looked over the statements we'd taken when Kyle Everly went missing. "This Oliver . . ."

"Work friend," I told him.

"Geoffrey and Douglas?"

"Poker and golfing buddies."

Ray got interested all of a sudden, and I only noticed because I knew him. Alert Ray and regular Ray would probably look the same to most people. Ray showed the statement that had snagged his notice to the FBI girl.

"Norman Blair?" he asked.

"Poker and golfing. Said they played a round with him a week or so before he went."

Ray did that thing that's always irritated me. He looked over my head and studied the seam right where the ceiling met the wall, like he was tuning into something you'd overlooked, weaving together threads you'd left to hang.

"Mind if we talk to these boys? Poker and golfing?"

To his credit, Ray has always been particular about permission. He doesn't step on toes or ignore protocol, has never made trouble that way. Instead, he'll bore in and figure out stuff you've long failed to put together and make you feel like he's shown up to do the job you can't quite do.

I had Keith and Gwen bring them in one at a time. They were happy to help and all that, couldn't imagine what had happened with Kyle. They were all standard-issue/regular-order interrogations except for the bit where Ray and FBI had some byplay with one of those boys.

"How you been keeping?" Ray asked him.

Norman Blair just nodded back.

"Funny to find you mixed up in this."

"Small world around here," the witness told him.

FBI girl said, "Tiny."

I got that old, queasy feeling Ray was onto something we'd somehow failed to notice. I knew from rocky experience the leading irritant of working with Ray Tatum was the fact that he was dialed in like you'd never be. Otherwise, he always seemed just plodding and ordinary, or even not quite up to ordinary but more in the way of awkward and slow.

I'd had my fill of his stuff in Georgia where Ray would wander by a case, have a look at the evidence you'd been chewing on to no good purpose and tell you who'd done whatever had happened and frequently explain why. It was a knack he had, but it wasn't somehow enough to make him a freak. He'd just seem like some guy who was up in your business more than you could stand.

Ray and I come at investigations from a couple of different directions, which makes for its share of friction, and on top of that, I've got personal cause to not like him much. Ray poached a girlfriend from me. That's my shorthand anyway. In truth, I'd only been out with her twice, and she'd said it was all just friendly, told me point blank she didn't have much need for a man in a regular way.

I was fine with that. Or rather, I'd decided to be patient in hopes that I'd charm her a little and her attitude would change.

Our second time out, we ran across Ray. Nothing involved or elaborate. We just bumped into him coming out of a place we were going in, and I did the proper thing and introduced Ray. I figured I could be collegial in the moment and run him down after a while, but it turned out she was aware of Ray, had noticed him around. He'd gotten into the habit of taking long walks with his dog, and then his dog had run off or died, and Ray'd had kept on tromping around without him.

My lady friend — Connie, her name was — reminded Ray that she'd met him once before on the trail out by the lake.

"Two of us," she told him, "and we'd seen that bear. Remember?"

Ray took his time dredging the incident up the way he always did. "Oh, right," he finally said back. "Your friend had purple hair."

"It's green now. Sort of yellow really."

"That might not work on bears."

She laughed, and I could tell by the tone and tinkle of it that Ray was already hitting her in a spot I was sure to never reach. And he wasn't even trying. That's what chafed me. I worked and planned and memorized patter, asked after stuff women were up to when I truly didn't give a hoot, and a guy like Ray could say one thing and make a woman giggle.

So Connie watched him go with more attention than I cared for.

"Where's he from?" she asked me.

I knew what she was getting at. Ray's an odd one all right. I was tempted to just say, "Earth."

Ray never even went out with her. It wasn't enough that he'd spoiled my thing and made Connie decide we were done being even friendly, but then he failed to take her up on all the overtures she made.

I wrote Connie three tickets after that in pretty rapid succession, and the boss brought me and Ray together and told us, "You boys work this out."

"Work what out?" Ray asked me.

He was authentically oblivious. I'm certain of that because Ray is authentically everything. He never plays at stuff.

"You snaked my girl from me," I told him.

"How?"

And the how was a problem for me, was always a problem for me with Ray because while I was calculating and strategizing and plotting the routes through life I'd take, Ray was just letting it all come to him.

It might have been because I resented him so that I was damn near plagued by Ray and only thought I'd gotten rid of him in Georgia. He'd finally quit down there and gone to Charlotte or somewhere, someplace where a guy who was down on humans could get down on them some more, and here I'd found a nice little country spot and Ray had fetched up in it. I hated knowing he was around and ready to take the shine off stuff.

Ray and agent Kate asked permission to see the bog where that Truelove had found the body, and I decided to carry them out there myself, wore my waders this time and made sure to only bring the one pair.

We parked up by the hunting lodge.

"Get a warrant on that?" Ray asked me.

"Didn't need one. They let us poke around. Nothing but canned beans and bourbon and mess."

"What do you think of that crew?" FBI wanted to know. "Douglas and Geoffrey . . . Norman?"

"Seemed upset and all."

Like usual, Ray was only about half listening. He pointed out a fallen tree, a big old barkless thing laying on a bunch of saplings.

"Wormy chestnut," Ray told us. "You could get a lot of board feet out of that."

"What do y'all know about the victim?" FBI asked me.

"Banking, corporate side. Wife and a daughter just turned three. Bit of a hound," I told her. "Where do you know this Norman Blair from?"

Agent Kate glanced at Ray who was taking the measure of a poplar by standing right beside the thing and eyeing it up its trunk.

"Besa," Ray said. "Whit's girl."

I got a twinge. It'd be just like Ray to make all this stuff fit together. Girl in a cellar. Guy in a bog. That bunch of suitcase people.

"She seems to know him."

"How?"

"Still working on that," Ray said.

I walked them to the soupy ditch that was left from where we'd pulled the victim out. There was a bit of crime scene trash and a couple of squares of plywood the techs had stood on to work but not a lot otherwise except for the stink of rotten leaf litter and a world of seepage.

"Any money problems? Gambling stuff?" Ray asked.

"Not that we've found," I told him.

"What then?" Ray was talking to himself by then.

Ordinarily, he would have wandered. I'd seen Ray do it countless times. He'd visit a scene and walk all over the place, but down in that bottom, he was a bit too hemmed in by muck to make his usual tour, so Ray sought out hummocks and managed a couple of orbits of the grave site. Kate watched him just like I did, seemed to know about Ray what I knew.

Ray eyed a lumpy spot of ground across the way. "What's that over there?"

It didn't look like much, just black muck a little more heaped up than sunk in. Ray headed for it, no easy trip because any ground that looked reasonably firm almost never was, so he moved like a heifer in a watering hole, just kept stepping and stopping until he got where he wanted to go.

Me and FBI stayed right where we were. We watched Ray have a look at that hump of ground and then swing around and have one at us.

"What?" she asked him.

"Got a watch over here." Ray bent over for a closer to it. "Nice one. Buttons and dials and stuff."

He scratched at some muck with a stick for a better look.

"Got an arm with it?" FBI asked.

Ray nodded. Ray said, "I do."

2

We decided not to kick ourselves for not finding that second body. We laid it off instead to one of those things no sane man could foresee and set up again in that soggy bottom, but we brought more planks to stand on this time and the ones with waders wore them.

Our fill-in lady doctor was on shift because of our regular doc and his swollen prostate.

"Who's he?" she asked me. Of course, she meant Ray.

She had a dead guy in a swamp with his head half cut off and a crew of forensic worker bees trying to get him uncovered along with every cop in the vicinity swinging by to see what was going on, and she'd picked Ray out of the swarm like they always seem to do.

"Nobody," I told her. "Guy I know."

Beyond taking some phone pictures of the corpse, Ray and FBI stayed out of the way, stood off to the side of the action talking only to each other. I could tell they were working through stuff, could see they had their own ideas, so in the circuits I was making, I started crowding them in time.

"Who do you figure?" I asked them.

"Who's missing?" agent Kate asked me back.

"Had a fellow wander off from a nursing him, but that was in the summer. This one's got a set of plugs. We don't see much of that around here."

"I've noticed," FBI said and then blew a nostril clean. I had to wonder where a gal like that was raised.

"Think we can sit in once you get him hosed off?"

I could hardly say no to Ray since he'd found him, so we all reconvened in the basement of the clinic where our forensic people work. We don't usually have the caseload to keep them busy full time, so they hire out for other stuff, but now our cold box was almost full — it only holds four corpses — and our regular doc was scarce.

I asked after him, and one his assistants told me, "Having a procedure."

"What sort?"

It was the fill-in doc who cleared things up. "Getting his prostate firebombed," she said and then introduced herself to Ray. "Believe you found him."

"Believe I did."

The doc gave Ray a leisurely once over and then shifted her attention to agent Kate who got kind of a snarly up and down.

"Now then," the doc said and turned her attention to the dead guy on the table. "He just about doesn't have a head."

He was certainly slit wider and deeper than would have been needed to kill him, and once the doc got her instruments in there and started pulling things apart, I could see pretty well to the back of that gentleman's neck.

"Knife or a machete," the doc said. "Pretty damn sharp. He's stabbed about all over. Got some punctures in his neck."

"Where exactly?" Ray asked and crowded in.

I'd never come across a human less squeamish than Ray Tatum. Plenty of cops pretend to it, but Ray has no qualms at all about butchered parts. Even agent Kate was hanging back. Gwen was almost out the door, and the doc's assistant was keeping his back to the carnage as he inked the dead guy's fingers.

"Come look at this," Ray told FBI, and she swallowed hard and stepped over. "Remind you of anything?"

She leaned as close as she dared and nodded.

"Nicked the artery here," the doc said. She fished the vein out with pliers and gave it a yank.

Ray picked through the tub with the dead guy's possessions in it. A watch. A ring. A car fob.

"No wallet?" Ray asked.

The tech shook his head.

Gwen volunteered from over by the door, "Maybe some kind of robbery."

"Bad kind," Ray told her and picked up the watch. "Here's ten thousand dollars right here."

After a while, the smell down there gets to everybody, even hard cases like Ray, so we all kind of filtered outside where there was a bench and a bucket of sand for butts.

"Happy to hear any ideas you might have," I told Ray and FBI.

"We've got no firm ideas," she said.

"Nothing that goes anywhere yet," Ray added. "Every damn thing's a loose end."

"Such as?"

They both ticked off stuff they knew in tandem, dividing the duty while they piled the evidence up. Evidence of what, I couldn't begin to say.

"So the dead guy in the house with the holes in his neck and that boy Curtis, you're sure they go together?"

"Some way," Ray said and nodded.

"The two in the bottom?"

"Don't know about them."

"And your girl from . . ."

"Moldova," FBI told me.

"She seems to know this . . ."

"Norman Blair," Ray told me.

"She say how?"

Ray shook his head. "Still working on it."

"Your people don't want this?" I asked FBI.

"Might, as soon as I can figure out what to tell them."

"Odd for around here."

I knew that wasn't true even as I said it, and I knew Ray knew it wasn't the case at all. People who've never spent much time out in the countryside prefer to believe there's something fundamentally wholesome about rural living. The clean air. The dirt underneath your nails. God's creatures running free. But that's not been my experience, and I've only ever worked for county police shops. Ray's worked in and out of cities of some size, and he's long held that country folk are the scarier sort.

"They don't believe in anything," is his take on it. "You know, like laws and civic duty, moral boundaries." If I'd heard that once from Ray, I'd heard it a couple of dozen times. "They're like livestock," he'd usually say, "with liquor and guns."

I sure understood the impulse to think that way. Only a fool wouldn't be worn down by the mess country folk get up to, which is usually some manner of ill-considered Old Testament vengeance or drunken carousing gone homicidally wrong. There's rarely any planning or thought put to it. Things just happen out in the boonies. People get shot by unloaded guns or get kicked into a coma. I once rolled up on a boy who'd been laid open with a mattock because his cousin had taken exception to him preferring Chevys to Fords.

So I knew Ray was talking sense, but his is the version without hope, with no faith in a higher power, no credence in

God's plan. I can't go quite that far, not that I personally have much use for Jesus, but my wife is a believer, and she includes me when she prays. She's convinced the good Lord has His intentions for us all, and I've decided to at least hope she might be right.

Ray won't even do that. His baby daughter drowned years back, and it changed him in the way a thing like that is bound to change a man. Ray isn't bitter, which is probably how I'd go. He's just not so charitable as he might be. He expects folks to lie to him and get up to devious mess, and the ones who don't are like the snake in the trail that chooses not to bite you.

"If you were me," I asked Ray, "what would you do with all this?"

"I'd bring in Norman Blair. Friendly chat, like that. Let the girl see him up close, and maybe something'll shake loose."

"She going to spit?"

Ray passed a moment thinking. "Almost certainly," he said.

I called Norman Blair myself, and he didn't sound rattled at all. More in the way of troubled and mystified and grieving, he told me, for his friend Kyle, so he assured me he was prepared to be accommodating.

Oddly, that Moldovan girl was a bit more of a problem, and Ray had to take a couple of runs at getting her in the building after I'd personally served Mr. Blair a cup of scorched coffee and ushered him into interrogation room one.

That farmer she was living with finally managed to herd her inside but only then with the help of his entourage. He had his Mexican, of course, and the biggest, hairiest Russian I ever hope to see.

I left Gwen to talk to the bunch of them, which mostly involved the foreign girl nattering at her and that big Russian asking for tea.

Ray and FBI rolled in presently. While Ray might be an incisive, perceptive sort, he's never once been on time to anything.

"Mind if we sit in?" Ray asked me.

Ray knew by then I was little short of desperate. No sheriff can have the news be largely about the bodies he's finding with no follow up in a reasonable time on who did what and why.

"We need a plan?"

Ray had a glance at FBI, and they both shook their heads.

So in we went, me first with agent Kate and Ray trailing, and bereaved Norman Blair looked ever so slightly more bereaved at the sight of them.

"Was it Kathy?" he asked.

"Kate."

"And . . . Roy?"

Ray nodded. He wasn't about to play along.

Me and FBI sat opposite Blair, and Ray plucked a chair off the stack in the corner and parked himself right next to the guy.

Norman Blair had a look at the one-way glass. "Who's out there?"

"Big Russian," Ray told him, "dressed like Peter Frampton. Do you own a pistol? A three-eighty maybe?"

Blair shook his head. "Two nine mils and a fifty. Don't care for the little ones. Why?"

"Your friend, Kyle," Ray said, "he got three-eightied." Ray touched his own head about where the bullets had gone into Kyle's skull.

"When exactly did he go missing?" Kate asked.

Blair was right in the middle of one of those useless hard-to-really-say answers when somebody beat on the glass from outside, and we heard a bit of yelling and a ruckus.

Ray and FBI were up and out immediately. "Sit tight," I told Blair and followed.

She'd spat for certain, and quite a lot. On the glass. On the frame. On herself as well. That farmer, Whit, and his Mexican were holding onto her from either side while the girl and the big Russian conducted between them a lively conversation. Gwen opened the door to the crew lounge across the hall, and the girl got steered that way.

She was saying a lot and quickly, only breaking for the odd breath, and every now and again she'd cross herself in the Catholic way as she spoke. Given her quantity of verbiage, what came out of that Russian seemed paltry by comparison.

"*Om rau,*" he told us.

Ray did the translating. "Demon from hell," he said.

Then it got worse, or different anyway because she caught sight of a photo that snagged her attention. We had our deputies sit for official pictures in their uniforms, high-school yearbook stuff that we'd frame and hang in the lounge. The ones who'd left, the ones still with us, everybody who'd passed through.

The girl seemed to recognize one of them, and she pointed and screeched and prattled.

The Russian boiled it down for us eventually. *"Om rau also,"* he said.

"Who's that?" Ray asked me.

"Keith."

Ray plucked Keith's photo off the wall and brought it down for a look, which put it in a good spot to get spat on, so it did.

"That's kind of a bad habit," I told Ray.

He wiped himself and nodded. The girl said a world of stuff, took a break and came out with some more.

"Muscle guy, right?" That from Ray.

I nodded. "Been here for five, six years."

"What's he like?"

"Tangled up in a thing or two."

Ray waited.

"Beat a boy with his flashlight a little while back."

"Why?"

"That was kind of the problem of it."

I never got an explanation that came close to satisfying, not from Keith, not from the woman who rolled up after it all started. Not from the review board that looked into it and sanctioned the payment the county made. Not from the boy Keith beat, though he'd been left gimpy and addled and said he couldn't remember much.

I do know Keith felt insulted, and he'd insisted he felt threatened. The boy he laid into was a buck all right and about as black as the Congo, but beyond wearing his pants low and his hat cocked sideways there wasn't much evidence he'd done or said a provocative thing to Keith.

He'd been picking up trash on the side of the road. His church was keeping a couple of miles clean. He had a stick with a nail in it and a bag, and he had his ear things in and his tunes cranked up like they do.

Keith kept his version simple. "Boy was in some danger of getting clipped, kept wandering out on the blacktop. Thought I'd stop and tell him to mind himself."

So he did stop, but the boy didn't see him or hear him.

"I gave the citizen instruction and due warning." That's the language Keith's delegate supplied, which translated in my head to Keith rolling out of his cruiser and shouting, "Hey, boy."

When that didn't turn the kid around (and he was just a big fourteen), Keith came stalking up behind him and poked him with his flashlight, was almost certainly giving instructions before the music got shut off.

Keith allowed he wasn't satisfied with the response. "He looked belligerent," he told the review board. "I believed him to be a threat to my person, and I responded appropriately."

Keith made a big deal of not having pulled his service weapon. "Determined to keep it non-lethal," he declared every chance he got.

He succeeded at that but barely. The boy was down and Keith was bent over on the roadside clubbing him still when a citizen stopped, a woman I happened to already know a little. Mary raises alpacas on a tidy farm in a bend of the river. She's an outlander up from Alabama where she buried her husband and sold her goods and then came here and bought a derelict spread and improved it.

She's thrived because she works hard and treats people decent, and she'll always tell you what she thinks straight out. I discovered that the hard way when we were making a push a little while back on immigrants and went out to her place to check the papers on hers.

She had all the stuff we needed. Hers were notarized and sponsored. I was riding with the squad that day, and I was handing her documents back when Mary declared she had a thing to say about folks like me and then spent about the next quarter hour saying it.

I tried to rebut her here and there, but she'd decided my sort probably got to talk enough and so wouldn't brook interruption as she delivered a tribute to her farm hands. She had three men in the fields and a lady in the house, and she cataloged for me all their virtues.

Then she capped it off with, "If it was up to me, I wouldn't be white like you."

So it was Keith's poor luck but good fortune for the boy that Mary rolled up on them. Keith claimed he was busy restraining the citizen and so didn't notice a pickup had stopped in the road.

"Heard the shot," Keith testified. "Swung around. Woman had a twelve gauge on me."

In truth, it was a twenty gauge, an old pump action, and Mary made Keith understand the next load was all his.

"Call that fool with the hat," she told him. I hate that went in the record.

"How's he still working?" farmer Whit wanted to know. That was a question you'd only ever get from a civilian. FBI knew better than to ask it, and Ray absolutely did too

Cops will set aside what's proper and legal when one of their brothers is caught up in a mess. It's an institutional reflex, effective and often wrong. Certainly wrong for Keith, and I did put the boy on traffic duty. He worked parking at the county fair and delivered the odd legal notice, but I'd yet to find work dull enough to tempt him to quit.

"No indictment," I explained to Whit. "Never went to trial."

I followed Ray and Kate across the hall and back into the company of Mr. Blair who set up a fuss about his schedule and his obligations, and Ray smiled and told him, "Almost done."

Ray had brought Keith's photo with him and handed it to Norman Blair. "Know him?"

Blair had a look and a squint. "Might be a guy from the gym."

"Is that a yes?"

Ray didn't put any spin much on it but still made it plain he preferred particular answers to particular questions he asked.

"I think Douglas knows him."

"Not you?"

He shook his head. "Seen him maybe a time or two. All those muscles. Kind of hard to miss."

"Help me here," Ray said. "I can't make much sense of this."

Norman Blair leaned forward, elbows on the table like he was more than ready to help Ray understand.

"Why does that girl out there — I'm sure you heard her yelling . . ."

Norman Blair nodded. "She seems upset."

"Is," Ray told him. "Upset about you."

"Why?"

"That's the nut of it, isn't it? Why exactly?"

"I'm sure I don't know, Roy."

"Then stick with me here while I do a little guessing."

Blair gestured like he'd be happy for Ray to do whatever he pleased.

"You don't look like the sort who'd keep a girl locked in a hole."

"I should hope not."

We were watching him dead close, me and FBI, and as best I could tell he didn't seem even microscopically rattled.

"But she's sure convinced you're in it one way or another."

Blair shrugged. "People get funny ideas. Bring her on in if you want to, and we'll get this straightened out."

"I guess maybe that'd be all right," Ray said and glanced at me like he was seeking permission.

I nodded and told Blair, "She spits sometimes. You might be wanting a slicker."

She came in with Whit and that big Russian holding to her by either arm, but they couldn't stop her from having a righteous fit at the sight of Norman Blair up close and in person. She confined herself to spitting mostly straight onto the floor, but she also raged at Norman Blair while the big Russian translated whenever the mood came on him.

"He is dog of Lucifer. From black stomach of earth."

The girl wailed and wept and lost her words. Everything started coming out exclusively as sobbing.

Once Ray had nodded at farmer Whit, they walked her back outside, and we could hear her moaning and weeping. She was putting on quite a show.

"Place her now?" Ray asked.

Blair shook his head. "Makes kind of an impression. I'd remember."

"How do you figure your friend got dead?" Ray had picked up another thread.

"I don't know. We've tried to put it together but just can't."

"You and Douglas and Geoffrey?"

Blair nodded. "Kyle always ran a little wild."

"He's got no record."

"I mean with the ladies. The crazier the better, and Kyle kind of liked them married. You know how men can get."

"This Doug's in real estate?"

Blair nodded. "Contracts and stuff. He's a lawyer."

"We've got properties we're looking at, and he keeps showing up."

"Busy guy."

"And your buddy Geoff, now he does have a record. And that boy seems to have kind of a kink."

Norman Blair shook his head like this was news to him.

Agent Kate told him. "Two assaults. One girlfriend, one prostitute. Performance issues, I'm guessing."

"I wouldn't know about that."

"Used a putter handle the first time," she told him. "A bottleneck on the hooker."

"News to me," Norman Blair said.

"But you knew he was bent." That from Ray.

"He's married. Got kids. How bent could he be?"

"The fed wolf," Ray told him, "still looks into the woods."

That stopped us. Me and FBI and Blair all glanced at each other. I've got an uncle who trots out stuff like that every chance he gets. He's not remotely my favorite uncle. The man's nobody's favorite anything.

"You know a Raphael Kempton?" Ray asked. "Might have known him as Steve."

"Context?" Norman Blair said. He barked it out like a man who was used to getting answers.

And he did get kind of an answer. Ray motioned to agent Kate, and she slid an eight by ten glossy across the table. It was a photo of Steve still mucky from the bog with his head cocked back and his neck laid open. You could see right up his throat to the roof of his mouth.

That was the picture I'd raced past when I was going through the stack because even in a clutch of ghastly forensic photos, it was the ghastliest.

I'd like to say we got the trash can over to Norman Blair in time. I'd like to say he spared my boots and failed to splatter on my trousers. I'd like to say it smelled like lilacs coming out.

I'd like to say him telling me, "Sorry, mate," made any damn difference at all.

3

Jan cooks exclusively from recipes and usually leaves a thing or two out, sometimes due to neglect but more often because she's got a quarrel with an ingredient. "Who has white pepper?" she'll ask, or "What does marjoram even do?"

Jan was on vacation in Dahlonega when we got together. I was in my dating phase, and the girl I was supposed to meet stood me up, so I ended up talking to Jan. She was touring around with a neighbor girl, lived at that time in Birmingham, and that first night I bought them burgers and then got Jan off alone. We walked around town and sat for a while in the park by the diving bell where Jan told me all about her loom, and I made to be intrigued.

Looking back, I was way too eager, but I'd hit the wrong side of thirty-five and had convinced myself that only a woman would spackle my gaps and divots. It didn't help that my mother kept running into my old high school girlfriend, Marie, who'd married the fire chief and had dropped a couple of kids, and she kept telling my mother how delighted she was with every stinking thing about her life.

Jan works at the middle school doing something administrative. She's tried to tell me about her duties, but she's one of those people who brings up her colleagues like I know just who she means. I don't ordinarily, so I tend to stop listening, which doesn't appear to matter much to Jan.

Increasingly, Jan seems down on human sexuality, and she claims to be on a crusade against vulgarity in our culture, which chiefly involves Jan getting offended and pulling a face. She reads a lot of detective books and often pumps me for what I'm up to, and ordinarily I've only got break-ins and traffic stops to tell her about, so legitimate bodies piling up made for lively supper talk.

"Spitting why?"

"Must be a thing they do. She's from way on over there."

"Where exactly?"

I drew a picture for her with my fork hand. "If London's about here and Russia's out there, it's in this general spot somewhere."

"Do they spit about most everything?"

"Doubt it. She was hot about this guy we'd brought in for a talk."

"They fell out?"

"That's the funny part. He says he doesn't know her."

Jan often tells me to try whatever has worked in some detective book she's read, too often forensic tests that haven't even been invented, but in this case, she went with an instinct instead.

"He's lying," she told me. "He knows her. Otherwise, she wouldn't spit."

Then Jan glanced at the clock over the sink. It was Tuesday, our conjugal night, and everything needed to be over with by close to half-past seven because Jan always made it abundantly plain she had better things to do.

She was good enough to indulge me in a wifely way, but Amish wifely mostly. Plain, you know. A duty performed with some dispatch and precision. At the end, she always patted my cheek and said to me, "There now."

I like to ride the roads after because I tend to believe it's about the only thing that'll keep me from raging around and flailing at home. I'll take the prowler down the business route and swing by all the hot spots and then loop out into the county and sometimes park on the roadside and sit. This particular night, I ended up in the vicinity of farmer Whit's place and stopped in the pullout where the road bends and just watched his house for a bit.

The porch light was on and the windows were lit. There was nothing at all peculiar about what I was seeing from the blacktop. Everything curious and unsettled was all in the car with me. I'm a go-along-get-along sort of guy, and I don't make any secret of it. The world's hardly perfect, and people are disappointing, so me and my crew just try to keep this boxcar on the rails. Consequently, I'm usually not the sort for scrupulous inquiry, and I'm ordinarily content that there's stuff I won't find out, things I'll never know.

Whit hardly seemed surprised to see me. I guess he was past surprise by then, and he said, "Sheriff," and swung the door wide. The girl was sitting on the sofa. Whit's TV was tuned to The Weather Channel with the sound turned down. There was a storm sweeping through some big, square state, and they were tracking it on the radar.

"Thought I'd see how things are going after, you know, today."

"She's settled back down if that's what you're wondering."

"Yeah, I guess, a little." I found a place to park my hat. "Where'd your Russian get off to?"

"He's Ray's mostly. Staying in one of those highway hotels."

"Odd bird."

Whit headed toward his kitchen and motioned for me to follow him. "You don't know the half of it," he said along the way. "He was some kind of secret agent."

Whit showed me his jug of Teacher's. He was having one already, so I nodded.

"Sure never seen shoes like his," I said. Whit handed me two fingers. I put it under the tap for a couple of drips. "Good he can talk to your girl."

Whit nodded. "What do you see for her down the road?" he asked.

"Got three bodies." I stopped to make a tally. "Yeah, three, and she's in it somehow, so she's going to have to stick around for a while yet. Have Ray and them got any theories on this?"

"Hard to tell," Whit said. "Ray's general feeling is people are a damn shame anymore. Got to figure what's going on here is some variation on that."

The girl came through the kitchen to get her some crackers. She said a string of stuff my way, and the best I could manage was, "It's all right, darling," back.

"Something about the ocean," Whit told me by way of translation.

"You speak it too?"

"A little. It helps around here when I need to keep her from mopping my rugs."

"We could probably find a spot for her if this is getting, you know . . ."

"Naw. Let's figure this out one way or another, and then maybe you can help her get home."

"Always the chance we don't figure it out."

"That deputy of yours with the muscles," Whit said. "Might want to start with him."

I'd been thinking about Keith, had personally gone through our files and pulled out all the paper I had on him. He'd come to us straight out of the army reserves, and he'd had a party back in that first, dumpy house he rented. I swung by to make an appearance. It was a sad do, as I recall, bowls of Cheetos and cans of Red Bull mixed in with the lite beer.

Keith's not a drinker beyond Gatorade and protein shakes, and he makes his own granola with (by the looks of it) silage and shellac. I remember he had a half-collapsed sofa, crates and stuff doing service as tables, a lot of free weights, a bench for lifting, and a massive, steel gun safe.

The door to the thing was standing open. Keith was proud of his gun collection like a gentleman of old might have hauled you into his study so you could get a look at all his books.

"You getting ready for something?" I asked him.

Keith grinned and said, "Can't never know."

Keith hadn't turned out to be all that much of an asset to the department because he seemed to be poorly equipped to sift and separate the right and proper stuff from the marginal and bad.

You run into that, particularly on the county PD level where the job, a little too frequently, is breaking up fights and riding herd. It's hardly the brand of employment that calls for moral giants, or even folks too terribly clear on distinguishing what's decent from what's trash. You just go where you're aimed and try to make whatever's happening stop.

Keith shot a Henshaw in the foot the first time he discharged on a civilian, and I know that boy. He's mouthy but no trouble much. He was around behind the Kroger looking to see what was available and otherwise just hanging out and being black.

Keith hadn't gotten a call but was checking behind the shopping plaza where most of my people would have given that Henshaw a wave and kept rolling along. There's no spite or meanness to him. The boy's just loud and pleased (on most occasions) to tell you a thing or three.

So he shouted at Keith, and let's allow it was probably something insulting and profane, but it more than likely came with that Henshaw's usual hoot and cackle. Keith slammed on the brakes anyway and rolled on out of his cruiser.

"Nigger this, nigger that," that Henshaw told me at the ER. "Then he's shooting right damn at me. Since when is that all right?"

Fair question. A round went through his foot and missed everything important, and Keith told us a bunch of rot about the peril he was feeling.

We ended up paying that Henshaw a middling piece of money and putting Keith at a desk for a couple of months, and that was about it. Then damned if he didn't pull his gun again, and this time he both missed the woman he was shooting at and killed her.

We didn't know her so well. That lady was somebody's cousin from somewhere, and she had a pistol she was waving around, though she'd not bothered to put bullets in it. She'd barely bothered with the pistol part. The way I heard it she was just trying to let people know she had it. She'd brought it out of her handbag with a bunch of other mess — tissues and pantyhose and gum and the like.

Deputy Gwen was there, had arrived ahead of Keith, and she was riding with one of our auxiliary officers, some deputized citizen with time on his hands.

"I pretty much had her," Deputy Gwen told me when I pulled her aside for a debrief. "The woman was on something and kind of off her nut."

"Did you feel you were in danger?" I asked her.

"Her perfume was getting to me."

"And the pistol?"

"I asked for ID, and she went fishing for it in her pocketbook. A gun came out but so did a heap of other stuff."

"She threaten you or Keith?" I asked.

Gwen shook her head leaned close for a private comment. "Think he's kind of scared of black folk, just between you and me."

Keith sure seemed ready to shoot them but not with terribly much accuracy. He hit that Henshaw boy in the top of the foot, and this woman had a bullet sail past her — accidental discharge, Keith claimed — and then she had a cardiac incident sitting in the back of Gwen's radio car. By the time the wagon came, she was already dead.

That whole business put me in a quandary because Keith might have been a fool, but the boy wrote more traffic tickets than the rest of my deputies put together. He'd pulled drivers for all gauges of infractions and hadn't shot a single one of them. I had stern words for him, naturally, took away Keith's overtime, and put him on prisoner delivery and courthouse duty and stuff like that. But once our quotas had dropped off as much as I could endure, Keith went back to work on the four-lane parked at the bottom of our blind hill.

So Ray's suggestion that Keith might have thrown in his lot with rooting-interest Caucasians didn't really come my way as a big surprise. While I didn't supply Ray with all the particulars, I let him know Keith had a history and was maybe a touch too invested in being pale.

While Ray couldn't say what exactly was going on and didn't claim he knew, Ray is the absolute opposite of a guy like Keith. Ray's got antennae and instincts, so when he told me, "This all feels a little like something racial. Tribal maybe at bottom," I believed I knew essentially what he meant because I'd also gotten stink like that off of Norman Blair and his buddies. Ray's might be better developed, but I have antennae too.

That Blair boy was so pleased with himself and calm that even a spitting foreign girl couldn't rattle him. What normal cowpoke goes through life like that? I decided to take a swing by the office park where he worked, even if it was going on ten at night, and I expected just to stop for bit and lean against my fender, have a couple of Pall Malls and a think. Then a swig of

Scope and wet wipes for Jan who hates tobacco a heck of a lot more than she likes much of anything.

And that's pretty much what I did at first, except maybe for the thinking, but then I caught sight of one of those fellows through a window upstairs. Not Norman Blair but his lawyer buddy, Douglas the real estate guy, and he was marching around and waving his arms, all red in the face and hooting.

Blair was up there as well and Geoffrey, and they were having a lively time of it, drinking beer out of bottles and shots of brown liquor too. I had to think they'd all let go of their dead buddy in the bog by then.

I allowed myself a third cigarette, and I caught myself doing some thinking, the sort of thinking I didn't normally meet with much call to do. I don't work cases as a rule. Not just me but my whole outfit. We get the odd whodunnit, but we usually hand them off to the state police.

We write tickets and manage parking for the county fair and stuff. We know most of the people in our vicinity who like to fight and pilfer, and these days we've got a whole perc-a-pop crowd who'll do about any damn thing to stay high. County cops used to worry mostly about alcohol and low morals, but now if you stop a swerving car full of schoolgirls, you're as likely to find heroin as not.

But we had three bodies and no narcotics, which was refreshing in its way, so I'd decided that, even with Ray Tatum, this was maybe a case worth working, worth flexing a few of my flabby muscles about.

When I pulled into his front yard, my lights found them on the porch. Ray had his music going like usual, that boy he liked with the horn.

I came up his front walk, I guess you'd call it. Rocks where he'd bothered to lay them.

"Problem?" Ray asked me, which I took as an invitation to climb the steps.

"Ma'am," I told FBI, mostly because she didn't like it and would give me the sort of simmering look I wish my Jan could muster.

The only seat available was on Ray's disassembled tractor mower, so I leaned against a porch post and asked Ray a question I'd been turning over. "What do you figure's at the bottom of all this?"

"Puzzle, isn't it?" Ray said.

FBI asked, "Have you pinned down the headless guy yet?"

We had. "Worked out of Richmond. Some kind of car broker. Old Corvettes, like that, and they had him running a little high-end escort stuff on the side. No convictions, but they seemed pretty sure about it."

I happened to glance in through Ray's door screen and noticed the boxy urn on his mantel. I got a twinge at the sight of it because the funeral home had put my daddy in the exact same one.

Jan was long asleep by the time I got home. I washed the cigarette off me as best I could and slipped under the bedclothes. Me in my boxer shorts and her in the nightshirt she always wore cinched up and buttoned tight.

I caught myself thinking of FBI just before I dozed. I felt sure she wasn't a "There now" sort of girl.

4

It was more spontaneous than anything.  He was eating.  I was eating too.  Ordinarily, I would have stayed at the counter and talked to Lem and Dot, but Keith was in a booth reading the auto trader and working on a cutlet, so I just marched over and parked across from him.

"Mind?"

"No, chief." What else could he say?

He sawed at his cutlet, forked a chunk of it into his mouth.

"Buying a car?" I asked him.

He shook his head.  "It was here already."

Enough chit-chat, I figured. "Tell me about the girl," I said.

"What girl?"  Keith went fishing for a biscuit underneath the greasy napkin in the basket.

"That foreign one the farmer's got.  It's pretty plain she knows you."

"From around the station and all," Keith allowed.

I sipped my joe and shook my head. "More than that."

Keith sopped his gravy. "I don't know her any better than you do."

"What about this Blair boy? Friend of yours?"

"Who?"

"Norman. Does banking or something."

He shook his head.

"How about his buddy Doug from the gym?"

Keith nodded. "I spot him sometimes."

"That's it?"

Keith shrugged. "See him around."

He ate. I sipped. We just sat for a bit.

"You got a thing about black people, Keith?"

Keith set his knife and fork down and wiped the grease off of his fingers. "What's up, boss?"

Now it was my turn to shrug. "Just wondering if I know you like I should."

"You thinking about cutting me loose?"

"Got no plans," I told him.

Keith picked up his utensils and went back at his cutlet.

"Is it because they're loud and dance and stuff? Spend all their money on rims?"

"We could all stand to try a little damn harder," Keith said.

"Ever met Doug's buddy Kyle?"

"Dead one, right?"

I nodded.

"Might have run into him at Jasper's."

Jasper's had been a Golden Skillet, but the franchise had gone under, and some boy had turned it into a bar. Boat shoe crowd from over by the college. The place had TVs and chicken wings and cheap happy-hour beer.

"We're kind of wondering what that crowd's up to. What do you think about it?"

Keith shrugged. "I just spot that boy sometimes at the gym." Keith slid out of the booth and lifted his hat off the hook. "We done?"

I've never quite had the proper knack for drawing truth from people, even people who give every indication they're ripe to leave lying behind. I did recall that Keith and Gwen had briefly had some sort of thing, so I decided to track her down and pump her for what she knew.

Their fling lasted maybe six weeks, started with too damn much rum. Buddy from the courthouse was retiring, and we all went to a party for him. They'd rented the lodge and hired Mitch and Sally who sang pop songs from the seventies. Mitch played the keyboard. Sally hit a snare drum and drank spritzers, and the gig was usually over when she couldn't remember the words anymore.

So it was the music a little maybe, but it was certainly also the rum that sent Keith into the parking lot with Gwen where they became 'involved', initially over by the dumpster and then again in the house Gwen shared with a cousin.

They tried to be sly about it for around a month while the rest of us watched them slip along through the phases of romance, from the giddy beginnings and powerful cravings to marginal indifference and conflict and then on to making up and fighting before calling the whole thing off. I think they did that last one three times before it stuck, and this was all in the course of six or eight weeks. By Christmas, they were sorta kinda speaking to each other again.

I tracked Gwen out to that tobacco farm where Ray and them had found all that luggage. There was a new girl working forensics and filing — Kirsten or Kristen, I was never sure which — and Gwen liked to take her around and expose her to fieldwork when she could. That seemed to be what they were up to when I rolled up on them.

"Is something going on?" Gwen asked me. "I've got the squawker cranked full up."

"You're good," I told her and nodded at the other one. "Hey, Kirsten."

"Kristen," Gwen informed me. "She found something. Show him."

Kristen had a proper tackle box from the homewares store where she kept her tools and samples. She opened the thing. It had pliers and trowels and rubber gloves and two tubes of VapoRub in it along with enough empty evidence bags to roll up on a massacre with.

She pulled out the one bag that wasn't empty and handed it to me. It had a watch in it. Smallish, like a woman's watch, with a cracked crystal and a dirt-fouled band. I could see the brand name just south of twelve o'clock, spelled out in Russian letters or something like it.

"Find this in there?" I pointed toward the barn.

"No, sir."

"Where then?"

It was Gwen who said, "Come on."

There was an old garden plot behind the barn, long unplanted and with the fences all collapsed, and a stand of woods on the other side of it. That's where we ended up. Not mature woods but a scruffy, viny patch of neglected hedgerow that had relaxed into a couple of acres of slash pine and privet and kudzu.

"What were y'all doing back in here?"

"You know, just looking around," Gwen told me.

"Snaky."

"Trying not to think about that."

"Snake won't care," I told her, and I was ready to bail, would have preferred that they'd simply pointed at this mess from the barn.

But then I noticed the flies, greenbottles mostly. "What are they after?" I was hoping maybe those girls had checked it out already and were going to tell me all about a possum gone to Jesus.

Once Kristen caught sight of those flies, she made an appreciative forensic noise while Gwen, for her part, just waded on over to see what they'd been drawn to. She's kind of a load for a female and so plowed a trail for me. Gwen still wasn't sure what she was looking at by the time I arrived behind her.

It was down in the kudzu, pale against the leaves and so unexpected and out of place that it was hard to see it right.

"Tell Kirsten to call her people," I said to Gwen.

"Kristen."

"And watch where you walk."

Gwen went wading back across, pretty much the way she'd come, and I just hung where I was looking at part of somebody's arm, or the bit anyway from just above the elbow to the wrist. The flesh on the underside was tattooed. Three stars, two in blue, one in red. The butchered ends were black with feeding flies.

I made sure Keith came, wanted to get him down in that thicket while our forensic crew poked around for other people parts. If Keith was tied up in this somehow, I needed to watch the man up close. Once he'd rolled in, I showed him the thing myself. They had that arm in a tub, and I walked him over to it.

"Look here," I said.

He grunted.

"They figure an ax," I told him. "Not even a sharp one."

"You thinking this goes with those suitcases?" he asked me.

"Don't know what I'm thinking. How about you?"

Keith glanced up toward the big barn and then back down to the thicket, did it with slow deliberation and a bit of a pained squint, less like he was troubled and more in the way of constipated.

"Can't say," was the best Keith could do.

"See if Gwen needs you," I told him and watched him lumber across the low ground like a front-end loader made flesh.

When the others showed up, I wasn't surprised because I knew Whit's Mexican listened to the scanner. He told us as much when we had him in the box, and he tried to make out like it was just civic interest on his part. Mexicans, I've learned, will fix their mouths and tell you nearly any damn thing.

They all came. Whit and Pedro must have put up a flag for Ray, and they brought the girl. That big, hairy Russian too. A couple of boys from our auxiliary force — raw civilians with

bossy streaks — tried to keep them up in the feedlot, but Ray
wasn't having any of that.

"It's an arm," I told him. "Here to here."

"Nothing else?"

"Not yet."

"Where did you search before?" FBI wanted to know.

"The action was all up at the barn," I reminded her. I
didn't tell her, "You were out here with us. You could have come
down here and looked around yourself."

"What's down there?" Ray pointed in the direction of what
looked like a grove of white oaks, stumpy, wind-gnarled
specimens like you get in weathered sluices sometimes.

"Woods, I guess. Haven't gotten there yet."

"Buzzard," he said and pointed. It was perched on a limb
of one of the trees.

"Come on, then," I told the bunch of them and led them
around the thicket and down the pitch.

It was about like I'd figured, a couple of dozen wind-
stunted oaks, some of them with limbs as big around as my
waist drooping onto the ground. There was hardly any

underbrush, too much canopy for that, but just lumpy tufted woods grass and dead branches and rocky places.

None of us saw the other buzzards until they'd hissed like they do and flown away, lifted out of the treetops with that whoosh of heavy flapping.

"Keep her up here," Ray told his Russian, and me and Ray and agent Kate continued down the slope. Another twenty yards probably, and we reached a natural swale where somebody had scattered — to judge by the trash — one bag of garden lime. It was mixed in with leaf litter that looked to have been turned over before the turkey buzzards had swooped in to scrounge around.

"That a foot?" Ray asked and pointed.

It surely was.

"What do y'all see?" Whit yelled from up the hill.

"Stay up there," Ray told him.

That didn't turn out to be a problem once Keith had wandered by. The Moldovan girl went banshee at the sight of him, leapt right on him and held tight. Keith's not courtly at all, not a man to be the least bit gentle with a woman, so I knew if he could buck her off, he would have.

She bit and she scratched and never really stopped yelling while Keith, for his part, lumbered across the hillside with her stuck fast to him until he stumbled, and she rode him to the ground.

We turned the whole scene over to forensics and moved up the hill to keep out of the way, and shortly Keith came to find me for a word. I can't say if he just wanted to keep his job or if that girl had rattled his conscience. All I know is he told me, "All right, I saw her once or twice." He pointed at Whit's Moldovan. "Out at some farm past Purvis."

"Tell them." I waved in Ray and Kate.

"It was Doug from the gym and that Geoffrey guy," Keith said, "A few other boys hanging around. Drinking beer mostly. Fooling with a goat."

Ray

1

That place was like a manufacturing memorial park. It had been buttoned up and fenced around, but everybody had long since lost interest, so the vandals had come through and busted what they could. Weeds were everywhere weeds could grow, between the buildings primarily but up on a few of the flat asphalt roofs as well.

"We even know what they did here?" I asked Kate.

We'd driven right in past an unhinged gate. "Stuff."

"Depozit?"

Kate rolled out of the cab. "Good a place as any."

We started by looking for tire tracks and trampled places, that sort of thing, and there was plenty of evidence of humans, largely in the form of trash. Beer and cider cans chiefly, but we found eight or ten empty tuna tins on one of the loading ramps.

Kate kicked at them and gave me her theory. "Cat lady," she said.

God knows there were plenty of cats around, enough to make me think the local people had given up on drowning kittens and had ridden out to this weedy, derelict spot to dump their sacks instead.

I'd brought my halogen lantern, but it didn't help much because those warehouses and empty factory floors were just too big and gloomy for us to light up in any useful way. They swallowed my beam. It stayed dusky everywhere, and I kept tripping on the odd carcass, birds mostly but one time something that had been a bear cub or a spaniel once.

"Can you catch asthma?" I asked Kate.

"This was your idea," she reminded me.

True enough, but I'd admitted to her that I was low on ideas at the time, which meant we were doing stuff that was only slightly better than doing nothing.

We'd pretty much gamed out what had happened in a general way, but nobody who knew the details was talking, so particulars stayed rare. It didn't help that Rowdy and his people weren't inquisitors of any scope and reach. They could sometimes get a suspect's pedigree down and ask him a string of specific questions, but they lacked the imagination to veer off and improvise.

Rowdy, at least, recognized and acknowledged that they weren't really up for the task, so he didn't bark when Kate finally put in for assistance, and an agent came over from Nashville. That seemed to me like a long way to send him until I got to know him a little and decided they'd probably shipped him to us because they didn't want him there.

His name was Gerald, and he was nearly as fond of Golden Corral as Pavel, which meant we could send them over there together and spare ourselves the ordeal. They had rooms down the hall from each other at the Hampton Inn, and those two got to be big buddies. One afternoon when I drove out to fetch Pavel, I came across him and Gerald on a feeder road taking a walk. Gerald was short and round while Pavel was tall and hairy, and they were chewing the fat as they strolled along like a couple of fellows from anywhere.

One of them had made a sort of career of killing people on orders while the other pursued and arrested folks like Pavel for a wage, but there they were deep in lively conversation between the Cracker Barrel and the Waffle House.

The idea had been that Gerald would serve as a conduit to Bureau assets and forensic talent, but Gerald's favorite bit of verbiage beyond "jiminy heck!" was "let's just wait and see".

He wouldn't pass anything up the line merely because we'd asked him to but usually required a couple of days of getting harangued by Kate who could often bring Gerald around to the view that what we wanted was necessary. It was only ever prints or blood work or Pavel money or something like that, but Gerald was one of those people set instinctively at no.

So it was all harder duty than it needed to be and not because villains are especially sly and clever but on account of how petty and territorial federal agents can be.

"How can a building this empty stink so?" I asked Kate as I played my useless light beam around the second warehouse we'd gone into.

"One of life's mysteries." Coming from Kate, I knew that meant (more or less) shut up.

There was no machinery left, just barrels, big steel drums with probably toxins in them, and everything else was open cement flooring splattered with guano. We could hear birds swooping between rafters, and a creature the size of a laundry hamper scuttled away from us and evacuated the building at the far end. I saw it briefly in the doorway and could have sworn it was a pig.

Rowdy and them had picked up some boys they'd tied through fingerprints and known associates to the bodies in the white oak grove. Three bodies, as it turned, cut in manageable pieces. Two guys and a girl, and she had a record. A murder charge in Estonia. She'd bludgeoned a woman to death with the leg of a chair, and there she was dead and hacked up in the Virginia woods. We had nothing much on the dead boys beyond scruffy and tattooed, but a few of the live ones Rowdy had corralled had mentioned the derelict warehouse that me and Kate were searching as one of their hangout spots.

Those boys hadn't owned up to anything much. Their lawyers had shut them down, but the way they were scarred and tattooed served as testament enough to the sort of stuff they'd been up to. I'd say "believed in" if I thought it went that far. Those boys had all been in and out of trouble, so their prints had popped, and in talking to them you could see they were supremely clear in their heads on what they hated and why. It boiled down to change primarily and anything that wasn't white.

Me and Kate had passed an hour watching Rowdy work on one of those boys, the fat one with the birthmark on his ear.

His lawyer was trying to shut him up and was succeeding at it mostly until Rowdy asked him, "So I'm supposed to live in a world that's wall-to-wall you bunch?"

The guy was shackled to the table but tried to stand up anyway. He showed his rotten teeth to Rowdy and shouted at him, "Already do!"

They were proud without cause and felt powerfully put upon and victimized without reason. It was the same with every one of them Rowdy and his crew rounded up. Their collective leading proficiency appeared to be getting inked. They weren't, as a group, much on hygiene, and it looked like they'd given each other haircuts. Their clothes were none too clean and often ragged, and they'd been living on various farms, usually either in abandoned houses or up in haylofts.

To see one of those sorry specimens with *Herrenvolk!* up his arm was to leave you not knowing what to make of this world anymore.

I guess they were loyal or maybe just stubborn. Most of them made use of one or the other of a brace of pro bono lawyers, a youngster just out of school and an oldster semi-retired. The young one knew too little to be useful and the old one too much to care.

"You don't have to answer that," was their favorite formulation.

The oldest of the herrenvolkers was maybe thirty-two. The youngest one was nineteen, and it seemed pretty clear the ones Rowdy had snared had been involved in some sort of mayhem, but they proved perfectly content to meet every accusation against them with a shrug.

I know the guilty tend to confess at length on television. I've seen plenty of those shows where the villain feels called to explain himself in detail and is pleased to entertain queries from the dogged police officials who have pursued him for forty-six minutes and run him finally to ground. That, of course, is not how it ordinarily works in life where humans rarely own up to much of anything outright.

"If you say so," is the closest I've ever come to hearing a confession, and that from a woman I all but caught dispatching her husband with a shotgun. I had to hit her with a coatrack to keep from getting dispatch myself.

"What do you figure is in these barrels?" Kate asked me. I'd been afraid she might.

I kicked the one nearest to us. It was full and heavy. The lid was crimped tight. The thing rang out through that warehouse like a gong.

I went and fetched my pry bar out of the truck. Probably two-thirds of the barrels we came across were empty or close to it, and we could establish that by tilting them a bit. As we moved through those warehouses, we took turns uncapping the nearly full ones. They usually had stuff in them that looked like machine oil and smelled worse.

It was too murky to see through, so I'd busted up a pallet, and we went around with a plank we'd stick down in the fluid. It was a long, slow job since, if that abandoned plant had anything in profusion, it was rusty fifty-five-gallon drums.

"You'd think somebody around her wouldn't stand for this," I told Kate once I'd slopped some barrel juice on me and it had made my flesh raw through my pants.

"Somebody who?" she asked me.

"You know. Do-gooders."

"How long have you been here?"

"About a year and a half."

"Know any do-gooders?"

Kate used to be the optimistic one, had a distinctly sunnier view of the world back when I first met her. She was younger, of course, and needed seasoning in just how dickish people can be, but even still she seemed hard-wired to be gracious. In the intervening years, she'd plainly done some souring, and it fell to me to remind her there were still a few decent sorts around.

"Like who?" she asked me. Kate was stirring about forty gallons of barrel swill at the time.

"How about Whit and Salvador? Nothing wrong with them."

"That we know of yet."

Then she opted for muttering about all the amateur sleuthing we'd gotten up to. "You ought to let him pay you. Wasn't that the deal?"

"You see how he lives. Whit's got no money to throw around on me. This all came along at a good time," I told her. "Happy to be busy."

I'd had all I wanted of watching my brother go green and die. Then I'd had to call his ex who took the news of his death alarmingly well and half covered her phone for a moment to tell her boyfriend (I guess), "He kicked."

I'd had a weird half hour with a lady mortician name Beatrice who served me coffee that tasted of hand soap and made no attempt to hide her disappointment when I failed to "let it out". Then I picked the furnace for him, wasn't particular about the urn, and didn't want any kind of ceremony in her chapel, which all served to color me for Beatrice as a heartless cad.

Me and Kate stopped at a loading door where the light was still good and the stink was tolerable. There was a trio of drums in the corner. I could tell by kicking that just one of them was full and so pried the lid off of that one, and Kate nearly shoved her board on in.

Luckily, she had enough of a glance to catch herself and tell me, "Ray."

I saw floating hair. The crown of a head. A yellow t-shirt through the milky liquid. There were a few streaks of what looked like blood on the cement floor that something had been eating. Rats probably, scraping it with their teeth.

"All right," Kate said, "I'm calling D.C.." It took some pleading from her to bring her Bureau boss around. I could hear that much, but we had a whole pile of legitimate trouble, so things swung in Kate's direction soon enough.

"Where are we?" she asked me.

I gave her landmarks and road numbers while Kate finished up with her boss. Then she alerted Rowdy who rolled up with Deputy Gwen.

"Y'all looked in all these barrels?" Gwen asked me.

I gave her my pry bar and told her, "Not yet."

"Got two techs coming from Quantico," Kate told Rowdy. "Bringing a bunch of state-of-the-art stuff."

Rowdy was good with that and passed much of the wait telling us about his chili.

"Jan's kind of a meatloaf and green beans girl," he informed us. "Thinks salt is a spice."

"I heard she knits sweaters," I said, just to be chatty.

Rowdy nodded. "Still kind of bad with the sleeves."

Word was Jan had a loom in their attic and a case, I think, of low-grade chronic depression, so she'd go up there and make a lot of square stuff to keep from having to face Rowdy and the world.

Rowdy called his forensic team in even after Kate had asked him not to, or told him to hold back anyway until her Quantico pair had arrived. Rowdy's regular crime doc had returned to duty in the wake of his prostate treatment, and I would say his ordeal had soured his mood if he'd not been cantankerous to start with.

Rowdy's doc was illustrative of what I've grown to consider the general trouble with people. We have a way of rarely rising to the moment. Something calamitous happens in our immediate area, and we still insist on being our lousy selves.

We had people shot and stabbed and hacked into chunks while life for us just bumped along. Some things ought to stop you cold, make you something better or at least something else instead of just some guy who stands around shaking his head and muttering, "Why?"

When it comes to (especially) homicide, I've never been big on why since it almost always boils down to some manner of passion or profit. People let go for a moment and do a thing that can't be undone. I'd been there. I'd killed twice that I knew of and wounded another boy we never did find. Every time, it was them or me, but that hardly makes it better.

We were still missing six women who'd come in through Baltimore customs with Besa. Rowdy had put out all the proper alerts, all the details he could muster, but he'd only raised a couple of false alarms and nothing else at all. We'd figured Besa might help some, but she'd straightened us out pretty quick. They'd all been on a plane together, and that was about it.

Those herrenvolk boys had nothing to say beyond running down wogs and mongrels. It seemed to be the only thing they were conversant in.

I had a cousin twice removed who'd gone from being a regular sporty sort to a druggy outlaw known for the quality of his weed. This was back when you could spend a year or six in the state pen for selling pot, and he did close to four and came out all muscled up and passably well-read.

I saw him shortly after his release, had never known him terribly well. We were both attending the funeral of my aunt, and afterward, at my uncle's house, I had a chat with him in the backyard where he listed for me, quite calmly, everyone he'd learned to hate.

It wasn't the usual "spics and niggers and ragheads" kind of thing. He'd smartened himself up in prison and knew the language of sociology, so nothing he told me sounded all that toxic and unhinged. He touched on cultural patterns and ethnic service provisions. It proved almost soothing to hear him explain why nobody mattered but him.

2

Those Quantico girls didn't roll up needing tips on being assertive. They tolerated Rowdy's doc for maybe half a nanosecond before they prevailed upon him to go elsewhere and right away.

They kept a couple of the local techs to help them with the grunt work, but they wouldn't get going in earnest until field agent Gerald had swung by to sign the official stroke-slash document the Bureau felt it needed signed. Kate had raised Gerald in the middle of a visit to an outlet mall near Chesterfield, and he was a solid hour reaching us, but those Quantico girls wouldn't budge.

They organized their van and waited, explained a bit about their equipment, and by explained I mean showed us their satellite uplink and then said hardly anything else.

Gerald apologized for taking so long once he'd finally rolled up. He showed Kate a jacket he'd bought along with a pair of brogues.

Gerald had turned out to be a clothes horse, but since he was built like a traffic cone, he tended to look exactly the same no matter what he wore. He'd get Whit or usually Salvador to snap a picture of him in something new, even if it was only a belt he'd strayed across or a fresh pair of argyle socks, and then he'd upload the photos to his Reddit community where a bunch of guys like Gerald commented on each other's outfits.

Gerald wanted to see the body in the barrel, felt like he had an obligation since he'd come clear from the outlet mall to sign his name on a work order, so Kate walked him over and showed it to him. Those Quantico girls had set up lights by then, which meant we were sure it was Curtis. You could make out his face down in the cloudy fluid.

At the sight of him, Gerald wheezed and quaked, and Kate escorted him outside sort of like they used to walk Elvis off the stage.

Gerald scrawled where he was told to and then headed back to his car. He had his new jacket and new brogues there to console him.

"How is he even an agent?" I asked Kate.

"Started in software. Kept getting promoted."

"Don't they know what the world's like out here?"

"No, not really," Kate allowed.

Those Quantico doctors needed help lifting the body from the barrel, and me and Rowdy got recruited. They gave us gloves, but that was it. We had to grab and grapple and hoist the boy up the best way we could manage, which put me an awful lot closer to Curtis than I would have liked.

Whatever he'd been floating in had some chlorine stink about it, and his eyes were open and cloudy. His t-shirt was bloody and perforated.

We laid him out on a tarp the docs had readied, had to reposition him twice before they were satisfied, and then me and Rowdy together hurried to strip off our gloves and get ourselves clean. One of the docs handed over a half-spent roll of paper towels when mostly I wanted to burn my clothes and forget I'd ever been born.

The larger doc pulled up Curtis' shirt. He had stabby slots all over his front torso, about a dozen of them. Each pretty much the width of a dime.

Me and Kate cleared up the mystery. *"Otverka,"* we both said.

"How do you get to where you care nothing about people? Just don't feel a thing?" I remember asking Kate later. It was probably half past four in the morning, and we were having a rough night of it.

"Care nothing about *other* people," she told me back by way of correction. "That's the trick."

"How do you even get there?"

"No idea." She rolled over and took the quilt.

The Quantico docs used the basement of the clinic with Rowdy's blessing, and once they'd cleaned up Curtis, me and Kate brought Besa in for a look, or rather she came over with her entourage — Pavel, Whit, Salvador, and Gerald.

Gerald must have taken her shopping because Besa struck me as more department-store American than I'd seen her look before. Skirt, blouse, cashmere -ish sweater and flats like a junior leaguer would wear.

She hardly shied away from that dead boy but instead eyed him up and down like she was studying a diorama.

"You see who did this?" I asked her.

Pavel translated. Besa said a fair bit that turned out to mean just *nyet*.

Rowdy had six boys in custody, all with their prints in compromising places, but they were doing a decent job of telling us nothing at all. A couple of them had done real time, one at Pelican Bay and another at Eastern State. We had three that were unreformed trash, came from families that had long histories of being worthless. Two of them were semi-local clans, and the third one hailed from out by Moundsville, West Virginia, so him and his people were known to police in Ohio and Pennsylvania too.

Number six was our ticket if we were going to have one. He came from Knoxville money, and his dad had driven up to bluster around for three or four days. The man acquainted us all with the sorry stuff that would happen to our careers if we failed to treat his Daniel honorably and fairly. He allowed he was big on honor and fairness, but he was inordinately quick with a threat. You did what he wanted or he'd see to it you were seven kinds of ruined.

He only quit telling me what sort of misery I'd know once I'd made him understand I didn't actually have a career.

Daniel Sr. was only marginally nicer to his son. In truth, they hardly seemed to know each other. Daniel Jr. would sit at the interrogation table, unshackled as a kind of courtesy, and he'd look at his hands or at the scarred tabletop while his dad bleated on about one thing or another.

We liked Daniel Jr. for a way into the whole business because he seemed afflicted with residual shame. He'd not gone the full tattoo route yet, had no ink below his wrists or above his collar line, and the stuff under his shirt was more drunk-in-Tijuana than white-and-mad-about-it. He had a unicorn, for Godsakes, on his left shoulder blade, and the foreign script he'd gone in for was Japanese and French.

Rowdy had decided he was probably gay because that's how Rowdy sorted and slotted people.

"Likes him a bit of rough," Rowdy told us more than once as if he would even know what that meant down on the ground where it mattered.

Rowdy was scared of homosexuals like Deputy Keith was scared of black folk. He probably barely understood what he got up to with his wife at home and was in no fit state to make pronouncements about the likes of Daniel Jr..

It was Kate's idea to question the boy well away from the lockup. She wanted him out of the PD and in the wide world that Daniel Jr. stood to lose. When Rowdy failed to bark, we borrowed his prowler, and me and Kate and Gerald took our boy into the field, specifically to the Dairy-O because he was craving a chili dog, and we sat at one of their picnic tables back in a puny sweet gum grove.

Gerald had worn a new tan corduroy suit along with his spanking new brogues. "If I'm honest, they're pinching," he told us.

Daniel Jr. had on the striped jumpsuit Rowdy made all his prisoners wear, and me and Kate (smelly denim) capped off a quartet that snagged some looks from the burger crowd. That worked for us since we wanted our guy in life but not quite of it.

We didn't pull out a recorder, and I stopped Gerald from taking notes. I just let Kate do what she felt she needed to do. The boy's father was a jerk, so it stood to reason that he could probably stand some mothering, and that was a tool Kate had in her bag. I'd seen her trot it out before. She'd go soft around the edges but not in a girly way, more like your night nurse handy to clean up your messes.

My job was primarily to stay out of her way or take some sort of jab at Daniel Jr. she could correct me about. He'd get the plush allegiance while I just got the elbows.

I'd say it worked on him except I doubt he even really required it because Daniel Jr. had been six days in a cell waiting on a circuit court judge. He wasn't going to get bond, but his dad's lawyer had filed a bunch of paper that had kept Daniel Jr. parked in the local PD with the drunks. His buddies had moved on to a fancier lockup where they got to watch a lot of TV while they waited for their bill of particulars to come down. Rowdy was holding them on something like unlawful disposal of human remains and trespass with criminal intent.

Daniel Jr. couldn't finish his chili dog. "Nervous stomach," he told us.

"Want a shake or something?" Kate asked him. He seemed not to, but she sent me and Gerald both after one anyway.

We could still see them from the order window where Gerald confessed, "I forgot my gun."

I felt sure he hadn't forgotten it but had not entirely cared for the bulge it made underneath his corduroy jacket.

I ordered Daniel Jr. a mocha mint because that struck me as his kind of thing, which should tell you how far from the usual master race specimen he was.

"What do you think she's saying?" Gerald asked me.

"Just trying to get him talking."

We took the long way back to that picnic table because I could see that Kate had drawn the boy out, and he was telling her something at length. That meant I got to tour the general vicinity with Gerald.

"Theory of the case?" he asked me and wouldn't let me shrug it off, made it plain that he was genuinely insisting on an answer.

"Some people," I told him, "have got a lot of free-floating anger, bordering on rage. You notice?"

Gerald nodded.

"Used to be folks knew how to keep that sort of stuff bottled up, but they seem to have lost the talent. Can't say I know why."

"What about him?" Gerald asked me and pointed Daniel Jr.'s way.

"*Qui vivra verra,*" I told him.

Gerald looked unenlightened.

"He who lives shall see," I tapped Gerald on the shoulder. "Tattooed right there. What does that say?"

Gerald didn't know.

"This world might be wider for Daniel than it is for those other boys. Could be he's a little less ready to leave it. Got to try to work with that."

We were nearly back to them by then, and Kate grabbed the milkshake from me because she'd decided to drink it all herself.

She pulled off the cap and licked the straw, told both of us, "Kip."

You take the crumbs you're given and, if you're working with Quantico docs, you might be able to build a biscuit from them. Those ladies didn't just process barrel boy evidence but went back through everything Rowdy's people had collected over time because they had the smarts and the technology to make better sense of all that stuff.

Their first full day in, they got more hits than Rowdy's crew had managed in a month. One was a Kip.

"Kenneth Boles Crowder," the little wiry doc told us. "Marine Recon." She handed his printed particulars over to Kate. Height. Eye color. Marks and tattoos. Nicknames: Rosco, Bleeder Boss, Kip. Honorable discharge and nothing since beyond a bar fight in Wheeling.

"Sergeant Crowder broke three noses and one tibia. Dislocated two shoulders," Kate told me, "and laid one gentleman open." Kate showed me a photo of the knife. "No felony charges. Some boys started up with him and came to wish they hadn't."

"Got a hooker too," the wiry doc told us.

We were down in the clinic basement with dead Curtis and his stink. Those Quantico girls had let Rowdy's doc hang around. He was togged up as well, cap and gown and mask and gloves, but had nothing to do beyond volunteering the odd correction.

He made quote marks with his fingers and said, "Escort."

Wiry Quantico doc sighed. "Whatevs."

She handed over to Kate a pair of charge sheets. One from D.C. and another from Raleigh. Pretty girl, even in a mugshot. Don't see too many Shellys anymore.

The top sheet was for petty larceny. Umstead Hotel and Spa near Cary. The second charge was straight solicitation. Georgetown Ritz-Carlton.

"Look who posted her bail." Kate handed me the sheet.

It was Steve from the bog, the guy with the floppy head.

3

Slowly and then suddenly doesn't only apply to going broke. Cases like ours have a way of fighting you right up until they don't. Then the ground shifts and the rock rolls on its own, the knot pulls loose, the wind comes from a fresh direction. Like the woman said — whatevs.

I was happy to let Kate pick through the details and figure how to rank them because she had honest-to-God training to fall back on. My experience was chiefly in arriving a bit too late to prevent some baboon from pounding a neighbor or tossing his wife around. Training wasn't a big feature. Smarts didn't much matter. You generally arrived slightly after you could have probably done some good.

Kate brought paperwork to the kitchen table and tried to make a show of eating, but I could see she was just pushing stew around. I have this game I play. Kate took a stand against turnips and rutabagas, so I keep putting them in stuff to find out if she has maybe not tasted them done right before.

"Got prints from Kip and Shelly too over at that one house," she told me.

"Which house?"

"Dead guy in the kitchen. Goat."

She ate the soupy parts and some of the pork, but her turnip chunks just traveled.

"Could this be just kicks?" she asked me.

"What?"

"This stuff. All of it. Bent jollies?"

"God, I hope not."

"I thought you'd given up on people."

"I'm down on them, sure, but that would be turning one hell of a corner. Hacking up a slew of people because you can?"

"I don't get the sense," Kate told me, "there's much rattling around in those boys."

"How about Blair and his buddies? Where are we with them?"

"Could be they were running things, but it's not like we can prove it."

"Running what though?"

She shrugged. "One of those master-race shithead clubs. They almost always end up looking like this."

"Y'all see this sort of thing a lot?" I asked her.

She nodded. "These days."

I watched Kate fork a chunk of turnip into her mouth. I thought I had her there for a moment, but I guess the metallic tang hit her hard because she shot me a look and spat the thing out, straight onto the floor.

We made an evening call on Whit and them, had Gerald haul Pavel over so we could show some photos to Besa and get her full responses down. We'd all decided against ever taking Besa back into Rowdy's PD, partly due to the spitting but largely because she'd stay shaken for hours after, and Whit made us understand that when Besa was upset, Besa liked to clean.

She'd stripped the wallpaper in his bathroom and had scraped the glue off with a spatula, leaving Whit with fixtures, a bit of tile, and lots of pocky gypsum board.

She'd done something similar to his kitchen floor in an effort to tidy up the grout even though there wasn't any actual grout and it was all just rolled linoleum. Worse still, Besa had 'cleaned' Whit's fancy walnut corner cupboard with a scouring sponge.

So we didn't hesitate to swing by in the evening if it meant keeping Besa calm, and Whit and Salvador were waiting for us with Besa on the sofa.

"How's things?" I asked Whit, Salvador a little too. He had on his lizard boots and his shiny pants, was dressed for a night out dancing.

Whit nodded in a wan and weary way, looked like a man half ready for a last meal and a hood.

"How's things with y'all?" Whit asked with emphasis, like that was the far more pertinent question.

"Starting to nail it down," Kate told him. That sounded optimistic to me. Kate dropped a bulging envelope on Whit's coffee table. "Got some people for her to look at. Places to see."

Gerald and Pavel came in chatting. Those two gentlemen had bonded over dinners at Golden Corral along with, as it turned out, the odd shopping expedition because Pavel had exchanged his usual Volgograd discotech ensemble for a Men's Warehouse three-piece suit and a pair of navy bit loafers.

Pavel had opted not to wear an actual shirt beneath his suit vest, so he was a vision in chest hair and tropical wool. Ankle hair too. No socks.

Gerald was the more traditional version, right down to a tie bar, so they looked like a brace of deranged twins. One was maybe an actuary, and the other one lived in a tree.

"Things are good?" I asked Pavel mostly.

Pavel nodded and described a dish he'd lately enjoyed, which sounded like trout almandine except with chicken tenders.

"Got some photos," Kate told him, and we retired to the kitchen so we could spread out on the dinette.

Gerald took special notice of Salvador's boots and shiny pants and drew him aside to quiz him about them over by the sink while Kate pulled a stack of photos and documents — our personal file — out of our lone, ratty envelope.

"I want to know if she's seen these people." Kate was looking at Besa but talking to Pavel. "And where."

Kate showed Besa, one by one, the crew. This was the bunch in the lockup, and Besa only recognized Daniel Jr. who didn't rate a screed, not even a little drool.

"Where from?" Kate ask.

Pavel and Besa had a back and forth, and then Pavel told Kate, "Farm."

"Goat farm?" Kate asked.

Pavel checked with Besa and then nodded.

Besa had seen Kip out there too, and it turned out she'd seen the woman as well, Shelly Marie Akers originally from Frederick, Maryland. Also Shelly Reno, and Kat Shelly, and Mary Akers from greater Philadelphia.

I'm not sure Kate intended to show Besa Norman Blair again, but she saw him anyway, and while she failed to spit, she spoke hotly to Pavel for nearly a solid minute.

We waited on Pavel to boil it all down, and he was aggressive about it because when he finally gave us the translated version, it just came out as, "Boss."

I sat by while Kate ran through all the questions she had for Besa, and she was thorough and took her notes, fielded a few inquiries from Whit. He was stuck on why? the way people get, especially decent civilians because the natural temptation is to conceive of even homicidal monsters as especially wretched versions of yourself.

Friction's the difference, as best I can tell. Regular folks bump up against their morals.

Police work, if you do it right, is profoundly unsatisfying because you have to slot amoral scum into a civilized process that observes their rights and protections no matter who and no matter what. There's no balance to it. That's the problem at bottom. Victims go into holes in the ground. Killers watch TV in Red Onion. How is anybody with a conscience supposed to come through that all right?

Kate was angling to get back in her boss's good graces, even if she wouldn't admit it, so she'd gone officious the way someone like Gerald probably would if he had the knack and the savvy. That's how you stayed useful. You followed protocol, collected your evidence, rounded up your suspects, and let the process roll.

So I couldn't even talk to her about it in any useful way since she'd decided to get invested in organizing justice, the kind that ends with a gavel and defendants with a bailiff on each elbow.

"What?" she asked me on one of our sleepless mornings, like four a.m..

I half rolled toward her and shook my head.

"What?" she said again.

I pleaded indigestion. Kate knew that was my bullshit fallback.

"What?"

"I thought that tea we bought would help. The bear on the box is wearing a nightshirt."

She did some fairly articulate nose breathing. "What?" Kate asked me again.

It's hard to shrug when you're horizontal, so I had to talk instead. "You know," I told her.

That wouldn't begin to do. "What?"

"It's this part I don't like," I said.

She'd heard my story more than once. I'd been thinking about him the way I do, just a boy behind the glass taking my usual twenty and giving me back my usual five.

He lived with an aunt, his father's sister. She'd brought him up when nobody else would. People around were aware he was slow and off. Not terribly much of either but enough to keep him out of step.

They called him Teddy. I never found out why. His given name was Simon Andrew Grubb, and he could read and take instruction, held down jobs at the grocery and hardware stores and sometimes worked late nights at the Qwik Mart.

It turned out he didn't sleep well either. His aunt told me she used to warm milk for him and sing him a lullaby.

*"Be Still and Know,"* she said, "but that stopped working after a while."

So he took a job at the Qwik Mart, nothing regular, just short notice when the boy on the schedule ran into some kind of problem and couldn't come. Teddy was there that night because the regular guy had met up with some girl, and they'd gone over to the Skate Ranch and gotten loaded.

"He must have opened the door," I told his aunt. I'd been sent to notify.

I was a Qwik Mart regular, and I'd go out most nights and drive around because I was immune to warm milk and lullabies as well. I had run up on Teddy a time or ten. He'd just be sitting in the booth, not watching the tiny TV and with nothing in hand to read. Instead, Teddy seemed to pass his shift looking out at the empty road and the vacant pump islands and listening, I guess, to the country music they played through the Qwik Mart speakers all damn day and night.

I'd sometimes stop in for my fifteen dollars' worth, usually about a third of a tank, and pay for it with the twenty I kept in the ashtray.

"Hello, sir," Teddy would always say and then give me five dollars back.

Late nights, when the store was closed, they confined the attendant in a booth on one of the islands. There was a slot for cash, so Teddy could take money and pass change back, but I'm sure most people paid with cards at the pumps, which meant the boy probably did quite a lot of just sitting and staring out.

He opened the door for the guy who shot him, knew him a little from around and must have thought (in a Teddy way) that would be enough. We had it all on security video. Teddy clinging to the cash box because he'd been told he was supposed to and taking a twenty-two round to the head. Dutch, the tweaker who robbed him, then helped himself to a carton of smokes.

He lived with an aunt as well. I doubt she'd ever sung lullabies to Dutch or heated him any milk. Dutch was part Irish, part Ho-Chunk Indian, and about a hundred and ten percent trash. He'd stolen the pistol he used from a preacher, had left him with a broken jaw and then had gone around trying to find somebody to rob because, as Dutch had explained once we'd scooped him up, "I'm sick!"

Dutch tried to tell us it was all an accident and he didn't know how the gun went off, that he'd just shown up at the Qwik Mart to borrow some money from the boy who was supposed to be working there instead of Teddy.

"We go back," Dutch told us. "Ask him." Then we showed him the security tape, made him sit through it twice, and all he had to say in the end was, "I'm sick!"

Dutch got better than he deserved. I know that for a fact because we didn't take him out and pitch him off an overpass.

I kept myself from stopping at the Qwik Mart for the best part of a year until one gloomy night I couldn't hold back any longer and swung by for my fifteen dollars' worth and then went to pay at the booth.

I tapped the plexi with my county badge, and the boy inside opened up. It was him all right. I'd interviewed him. Drunk at the Skate Ranch with some girl.

I only punched him once. Short and sharp, flush between the eyes. I'd turned myself in at the station house by dawn.

"What's your plan then?" Kate asked me because she could be certain I wouldn't have one.

My plan was to start with a scoured earth and put different people on it, which is not in any practical sense a plan.

"I say we sit down with the county prosecutor and see what's possible."

"Right," I told her.

"Look at what the docs have pinned down in just the past couple of days."

"Right."

"Conspiracy. Kidnapping. Assault. Before you even get to homicide."

"Right."

"Those boys'll start flipping. You know they will."

I grunted.

"The whole lot'll rot inside."

"And Blair?" I asked her.

She made a noise I recognized. The one that meant "we'll see".

Rowdy himself called us in at half past nine in the morning because a trooper had scooped up Shelly Marie Akers. She was riding on the shoulder of the interstate, going about twenty-five.

We could see why well enough once we'd arrived at the station house. She was coming down off something and was still twitchy and glassy-eyed.

"Talk to her yet?" I asked Sheriff Rowdy.

"Tried, but she wasn't making sense. Boy found this in her car." Rowdy showed us a sizable tactical knife they'd tagged and bagged along with a sheath the length of my boot. The blade was serrated on top and had some kind of black oxide coating so you could slip up, say, on a pimp at night and nearly cut off his head without any glare.

"I was thinking maybe girl to girl." Rowdy told that to Kate primarily because he was precisely the sort of guy to believe women had a secret code.

Kate carried a coffee in for herself along with Rowdy's file on Shelly Akers, that knife in a bag and a prickly attitude.

"What are you on?" she asked and dropped her stuff onto the table.

Shelly Akers shook her head and rubbed her wrists.

"Coke? Meth? X? What?"

Shelly Akers shrugged, couldn't seem to conceive of why it mattered.

"You good to talk?"

The woman nodded, rubbed her wrists some more.

Kate opened the file and sifted through the contents, mostly faxed copies of documents and glossy stacks of forensic photos. She fished out a shot of Steve the pimp laid out on a tarp down at the bog.

"Friend of yours?" Kate asked and slid the photo across the table.

The woman had the reaction a human ought to have. She groaned and shuddered and shoved it back toward Kate.

"Here's a better one." Steve was hosed off on a table but no less butchered and dead.

Shelly Akers opened her mouth and noise came out. You could have readily taken it for grieving. She showed Kate burn scars on both of her lower legs. "He did all this," she said.

"There's your motive," Rowdy told me from back of the glass, as pleased as he could be.

"Haven't even had a good look at this yet," Kate said of the knife in the bag. "A lot of channels and grooves. Am I going to find any blood?"

Shelly Akers did that sinking, collapsing thing suspects sometimes do when the truth of this world hits them and hope vents off and escapes. She got smaller, slouchy, borderline despondent.

"Where's Kip?" Kate asked.

Shelly Akers shook her head. "Don't know."

She had nothing to say about Norman Blair beyond that he'd been a client, though she was pleased to list assorted offenses Clifford and Steve had committed against her — assault in about every flavor it can come.

Kate asked about the herrenvolkers, and got back, "Fools," and a snort.

Eventually, Shelly Akers provided near-Dickensian versions of the carnage she'd done. She told why and how and spoke in detail of the training she'd been given, but she wouldn't let Kip take any measure of the blame.

"All me," was what she said, and she told Kate she'd meant to kill herself once she'd heard we were looking for her. "Couldn't do it," she said. "Isn't that some shit?"

Near the end, Shelly Akers grew tired and melancholy and started talking about a man she'd known out in Oregon, a timber executive named Sheldon who'd always treated her right.

That's when Deputy Gwen came in to find us and pass along the news that some civilian auxiliary volunteer — the sort with a light on the roof of his Fiesta — had been checking on the Big Lots, an abandoned shell of a place out of business for years.

"Dead guy in the parking lot," Deputy Gwen told us.

"We know who?" Rowdy asked.

"Kenneth Boles Crowder," Gwen told him.

"That's Kip, right?" Rowdy wanted to know.

I nodded. "Homicide?"

"Shot himself," Gwen told me.

It seems nerve had been no problem for him.

4

Out on that part of the four-lane, all of the retail rot and clutter had run the other way, so it was just the Big Lots plaza, a Pilot station, and a fenced-in compound where they took all the LP tanks for a coat of paint.

The Big Lots parking lot was superstore sized and was all trashed up and weedy, not really a place I'd think to go to shoot myself in the head. I rode out there with Rowdy who spun his theories at me along the way.

"You heard those boys," I finally told him. "There's no world they want to run, just people they'd be pleased to kick around and break to pieces."

Rowdy shook his head and grunted like I'd suspected he would because Rowdy always liked his culprits to be up to something grand. They couldn't be just drunk and stupid, sober and stupid, mean for meanness' sake. They all had to be scheming because Rowdy needed some kind of malevolent angle. He'd resist a twelve pack of Woodchuck Cider being the fuse for some brand of mayhem, but Rowdy was always ready to wrap his arms around a caliphate.

Kip was leaning against the concrete base of a light pole in the middle of the lot. Some enterprising soul had sawed the pole open and stripped out all the wiring, and Kip had splattered onto the exposed junction box. He'd used a Colt revolver, a .45, and it had more than done the trick.

His driver's license was in his lap, a thoughtful touch for whoever might find him, and his Dodge sedan was parked well clear and over by the store.

Rowdy's doc drove out by himself in his wagon, not his forensic truck but his ancient Volvo, a big boxy one he'd painted brown with (by the looks of it) a brush.

He tugged on his purple gloves in a drama-club way and then bent down for a close look at the wound, pulled out his flashlight and unsleeved a swab. He sneezed twice the way Rowdy's doc always seemed to and said, "Well," like he usually did.

I'd half decided the man was allergic to exsanguination.

Rowdy got nostalgic in fairly short order and had a long look at the Big Lots with its front windows all boarded up.

"Used to come here and buy yarn. Big ol' boxes of it. Worst colors you ever saw," he said. "Bought some towels in there once, wouldn't dry a duck."

Norman Blair and his buddies Douglas and Geoffrey had submitted to a couple of casual chats and then had made it plain that we could do all our talking to their lawyers going forward. And these were the kinds of lawyers with manicures and two-thousand-dollar suits instead of our local crew with neckties that barely reached their navels.

I knew they'd walk, or something close to it. I'd seen this sort of thing play out before. The boys in the jumpsuits with tattoos up to their earlobes tend to stay too high and loaded to remember anything much and are always looking for you to tell them what exactly they'd best say unless, of course, they've decided that going inside is the better option for them.

A roof, a bed, a chapter of the Aryan Brotherhood, hot food, a job in the laundry, free weights in the yard. Depending on where you're standing, that might not sound too bad.

We had a fair idea of who'd done what, a good feel for the dynamics, and sound reason to believe the herrenvolker would probably get stuck with it all. We had some accessory action on

Norman Blair, but that was pretty much the limit of it, and if Douglas and Geoffrey kept their mouths shut, they'd walk away from everything.

The Quantico docs gave us all they could find, and Rowdy passed it up the ladder. The county prosecutor was already knee-deep in pleas, so that stuff was all gravy for him. Rowdy, as kind of a sop I guess, left dealing with Norman Blair to Kate, and she took me along once I'd sworn up and down I wouldn't get up to anything vengeful and foolish.

It was Kate who decided to swing by Whit's before we visited Blair because Whit had checked in to tell us that he and Salvador together were having a chore of a time explaining American jurisprudence to Besa.

"She's doing a lot of crying," Whit told us. "I'd almost rather she cleaned my house."

Besa had dried up by the time we got there. She was halfway through a sleeve of saltines, and she gave us some hot Moldovan commentary and then panted a little and cried.

I noticed Pavel had put a shirt on under his tropical weight Men's Warehouse vest, not a dress shirt so much as the manner of blouse a buccaneer might wear. He'd also given up his blue bit loafers and gone back to his sneakers. No surprise there. Pavel seemed the sort who needed his toes to breathe.

"The foolish man," Pavel told us, "seeks happiness in the distance."

We nodded or something.

"It is better to get wool from a scabby sheep than nothing at all."

We waited. When Pavel got on a proverb jag, that's about all you could do.

In time, Kate joined Besa at the table and gave her the dirty truth about American criminal law with an emphasis on reasonable doubt and the assumption of innocence.

Besa and Pavel got emphatic over a few eastern bloc maneuvers that they believed would serve us well for Blair. Apparently, a tiled room was what we needed with an open drain in the floor.

Besa mostly wanted to rage and vent, and Kate knew enough to let her, which meant we sat around Whit's kitchen for nearly an hour until Besa was about spent. Or until anyway she hit a lull, and that's when Kate decided to tell her that we were off to inform Norman Blair about his accessory charges. She described the brief time he would possibly do and the spoilage his professional life might suffer as if either of those could come within sight of enough.

Besa said something that sounded like 'chef', came out with it three or four times.

Pavel translated. "Boss," he told us. "Boss," he said, and "Boss."

We saw them, of course, because they followed us over in Gerald's big white sedan.

"What do you think they're hoping for?" I asked Kate.

"Better not be much," was all she said.

The plan we'd hatched with Rowdy was that we'd ride out and tell Blair to surrender come morning. We'd say his girlfriend had implicated him and he had charges to answer for. We hoped he would worry in the night and maybe try to destroy some evidence or, better still, go out to the Big Lots or somewhere and pull a Kip on himself.

It was evening by the time we reached the office park, crowding seven o'clock, so the place had largely emptied out, but lights were still burning in the bike room.

As I eased in to park, Kate told me, "There he is," and pointed.

I spied him in the window where I'd seen him that first evening. He was slick with sweat, earbuds in, peddling like a madman.

We waited for Gerald and them to roll up so we could see what they intended and either leave them out in the lot or send them home.

Kate peered into the car. "Got to stay out here if you're staying." She was talking mostly to Pavel, I imagine. I sure would have been because you don't want the wetworks guy all up in your stuff.

He said something in Russian I couldn't quite hear but then he translated, telling Kate in his usual Volga rumble, "The law is hard, but it is law."

Mason was out in the upstairs corridor, precisely like before. This time he was eating a kiwi and hadn't bothered to peel it but was having it the way you'd eat an apple, hairy hide and all.

"Oh, hi," he said.

Kate pointed down the corridor.

"I'm supposed to tell you Mr. Blair requires a warrant."

"Are you now." Kate pushed past him, and I followed her into an empty room. No sweaty, chinless investment counselor. His bike seat was still warm and damp.

Mason came in behind us. "I'm supposed to . . ."

"Where did he go?" Kate asked.

". . . tell you Mr. Blair requires . . ."

Kate waved him off and stalked back the way we'd come. Mason followed her down the hallway.

I stepped over to the window just in time to see Norman Blair slip into the parking lot. Whit and them were all out of Gerald's sedan taking the air when Besa recognized the *om rau* among them in gym-room casual wear.

Besa pointed and screeched and said a rapid string of emphatic Romanian stuff. In her rage, she closed on Norman Blair, had very nearly reached him before Pavel managed to grab her from behind. He picked her up and set her aside. Then (I guess) because he was handy, Pavel wrapped his arms around Norman Blair and picked him up as well.

Pavel attempted what looked, from where I stood, like a chiropractic adjustment, what you'd do to a man complaining about some stiffness in his neck. He was quick and decisive, as efficient as could be, and then let go of Norman Blair who piled up on the asphalt.

Pavel was back alongside Besa by the time Kate reached them. She poked Norman Blair with the toe of her boot and then went searching for a pulse before she swung around and found me in the window.

"Holy hell," I believe I told myself, along with maybe, "Jiminy heck."

Kate called the Quantico docs, and the larger one informed us she'd seen a world of dead humans but never one extinguished quite like Norman Blair had been.

"Who saw what happened?" she asked us generally.

"I did." I pointed at my window. "Looked like he tripped and landed funny." That was what I'd settled on.

One of the others could have jumped in and offered up a contradiction, but they all claimed to have been looking somewhere else.

"Could be," I suggested to the Quantico docs, "he was going for the girl."

Pavel had a thing to add to that. It was *"Da."*

"What's he wearing?" the skinny doc asked as she gave Pavel a once over. It came out like she'd meant to think it but somehow said it aloud instead.

"Boglioli," Gerald told her. "Sixty percent off."

Pavel said a phlegmy thing in Russian and then offered up the English version. "The cat," he informed us, "always knows whose meat it has eaten."

I both didn't understand it and knew exactly what it meant.

~~~

Things have a way of going clerical. You don't need to want or allow it because it just happens like all your stuff getting wet in the bottom of a boat. There's no effective cure for it, no precaution you can take against your percolating outrage becoming merely ink on paper and lowlives allocuting without owning up to a thing.

I've sat in an awful lot of courtrooms and have heard plenty of sentences read, and I've decided justice is hardly worth the bother. Everything broken stays that way. Nothing satisfies.

We had no trials, just pleas, and I can't blame our county prosecutor because if those herrenvolker were nothing else, they were loyal to each other. Even Daniel Jr. got with the plan.

There was plenty of forensic evidence — circumstantial but fairly damning — and a slew of corpses to generate outrage with, but the county guy was sensible where it came to local jurors. I'd been in the area for a couple of years, and the people there were nothing special. Ignorant, suspicious, full of self-pity and eager to seethe given half a chance.

You couldn't really hope to convince twelve of them of any one true thing. They weren't built that way, and the prosecutor — raised eight miles from the courthouse — knew it.

Whit stayed upset. He had a salt-of-the-earth investment, was a decent man, a proud dirt farmer, and he tried to convince us all that local folks would almost certainly reach the proper verdict.

"Just put it in front of them," he kept saying. "They'll figure out what to do."

Salvador knew better because he'd been Mexican in these parts for a while and seemed to think, like I did, that the righteous stuff was all veneer.

So Whit would say, "They'll figure it out," and Salvador would only smile. He knew well enough they'd figured it out already.

So the prosecutor took pleas from the herrenvolker who all got decent time, and one of Shelly the escort's former clients paid for an Arlington attorney to contest the woman's incriminating statements and tangle with our local guy over assorted lesser charges that might suit.

Norman Blair took an awful lot of the weight since he was conveniently dead. His pals Douglas and Geoffrey put their mutual friend Kyle on him and described how Blair had walked up behind him and shot him twice in the head.

There was some grumbling, of course, among people upset that those boys and that whore would eventually get out. Nobody complained much about the two who'd never go in in the first place. Officially, nobody ever located those six missing refugee girls, but a dancing Mexican I'm acquainted with told me on the sly that he'd heard those girls had washed up on an alpaca farm in a bend of the river. It seems they'd decided to settle in and take America as they found it.

Two men came for Pavel. They wore suits and carried proper briefcases. The one who finally cornered me had on the whitest shirt I've ever seen.

"You brought him down here?" he asked me. "You did this?"

For a second there I thought I might catch him up on the particulars of the matter, explain how we'd been looking for a translator, not a wetworks guy.

"See what you're making us do?" he said. We were standing outside of the PD where that fellow's associate was ushering Pavel onto the back seat of a gray sedan. "Got to move him. Start all over."

He clearly wanted an apology or some display of shame. Instead, I told him, "Be sure and put him near a Golden Corral."

I remember that night sitting out on my porch, glasses empty and music off. A nighthawk was chirping and that goat was rolling around in a patch of dirt. We had a sliver of moon and a spot of breeze, but I knew none of it would matter.

"I already can't sleep," I told Kate, "and I'm not even in bed."

Salvador

"Why did she have to show up here?" Whit still asks me now and again. He did it a couple of times a day for a while.

I tell him, "Fate." I tell him, "I don't know." Sometimes I tell him that thing from Pavel, the one the sheriff got all wrong when he was talking to the Richmond paper. "That cat's damn sure," the big fool told them, "it's eating your lunch in the woods."

Things are pretty much back to regular now. Me and Whit are clearing land these days and keeping fences mended. We've all but rebuilt Whit's power lift, put new tin on his house, and there are stretches when we talk the same old rubbish and little else.

Ray had us all over to see his brother off. It was him and his girl, me and Whit and Besa. Gerald the Bureau man even came out, and Ray must have made some kind of peace with Rowdy. He showed up with his wife, and she brought everybody a homemade sweater. They were all in road-crew colors, fit like ponchos, had weird sleeves, but that was sure ambitious for a party favor.

Ray had picked a spot for his brother. He lives in one of those blind horseshoe valleys about ten miles west of the interstate where you have to go out the same way you went in. He'd found a bald on one of the hilltops where people had been buried, but the fence was long down around them, and the stones were all weathered and busted.

It was a chore to get up there, plenty of underbrush and prickly thickets to wade through, and the old pasture was steep and rocky, but only Gerald complained. Ray had told him "funeral service", so Gerald had worn the wrong kind of shoes.

The goat came along too. I had one for a while, and mine was always up for an outing. Ray's goat would see something he wanted to munch and wander off to do it, but then he'd hustle up and find us all again.

It was windy on that hilltop and misty off and on. The most recent occupant, from what I could make out, had died in 1928. "Angels Came" is what the headstone said and then some stuff about Jesus that time and rain had shallowed and worn away.

Ray had his brother in what looked like one of those things you put sugar or flour in. It wasn't any fancier, that's for sure, but just a tin box with a lid. I think he rattled some, the brother, like there was bone in with the ash, which I tried not to hear as we were walking. Who wants to end up clacking like that?

"All right, then," Ray said once we'd gathered upwind, all but the goat who was having a go at a laurel across the hillside. "My brother was kind of a jackass," Ray told us, "and taught me everything about it I know, so to the extent I've rubbed y'all wrong, here's the guy who caused it."

I remember standing there thinking you can be certain you're finally part of the furniture when people see fit to invite you to something like this.

"He blew up everything there near the end," Ray told us, "and I never thought I'd say this, but I'm glad he came to me." Ray was talking to the box by then and working at the lid. "Enjoy the view, brother."

Ray shook and dumped his brother out, and he spread on the breeze and dusted the pasture grass. We all stood and mumbled amen-ish stuff and thought about — at least I did — how a man isn't ever so much that he can't get made to fit inside a hopper no bigger than you'd pour some sugar in.

I'm pretty sure nobody had counted on Besa singing. She'd made quite a lot of racket since we'd known her, but not much of it had been musical, so me and Whit were particularly surprised.

You could tell it was a sad song, and she had the voice for it, pure and tuneful. Even the goat seemed to listen with more than the usual notice stuff gets from goats.

For my part, I stood there wondering about the mystery that was Besa who'd come halfway across the planet chasing some sketchy promise of work. She didn't know English and hadn't picked up much her whole time here, so what did she think would happen, how was she figuring this new job would go? We never could get her to talk about everything she'd left behind. No matter how hard me and Whit worked to pick up some Romanian, Besa wouldn't play along, refused to fill the holes.

We had a meal at Ray's house, some kind of stew, wine out of a box, and a pound cake with a considerable sad streak through it. Besa put on her sweater and, but for the roof, you could have seen her from outer space. Sheriff Rowdy shared with us the news that he'd sent his big deputy packing.

"I thought I had a use for him," Rowdy said. "Had decided I could stand to keep him on, but I got to thinking the bad stuff in him couldn't help but taint the rest. That's how it works all over, isn't it? Once the poison takes hold, it creeps."

Rowdy considered his plate like a man about to uncork additional weighty pronouncements, but instead, he stirred his stew and asked Ray, "Are these things turnips or what?"

It needed Kate and Gerald together to get Besa's papers straightened out, and Kate was back in D.C. before the visa or whatever it was came through. Whit bought Besa a suitcase and proper traveling clothes and packed her two full boxes of saltines. We rode up together in the small hours — me and Whit and Ray and Besa and Bootsy — and got to Dulles before the traffic had grown thick.

Kate met us there all FBI'd up, in her suit and with her hair pulled back. She must have felt like she needed that look to persuade the right people to let Besa on her plane because Besa's circumstances were so odd and her papers were so peculiar. The shabby ex-cop, the dirt farmer, and the Mexican probably raised some flags as well.

We were a crew all right, and we stood there in that big terminal waiting while Kate talked to one guy in a jacket and then another who'd have chats on their walkies and chats on their phones. Then they'd come back to Kate and she'd talk to them some more.

Suddenly Besa needed to be at the gate, and the men who'd been holding her up acted like the delay was all her doing. One of them grabbed her by the elbow while she tried to hug us all, and then they hustled her through a doorway marked DO NOT ENTER! in four languages — none of them even close to Romanian — and the girl was gone.

We were some kind of quiet all the way home. Stopped for gas once, and while Whit did the pumping, me and Ray just wandered around. Not together. He went one way, and I ended up down by the roadside. We were probably both trying to bundle stuff up and figure how best to pack it away.

I knew what I'd do, had laid it out in my head. I'd wear my maroon suit with the stripes and the lizard boots I'd had made special. The bolo my uncle had left me and his beaver cattleman too. I'd call my girls to get a read, see which of them was eager, and I'd probably wax the Cherokee before I picked her up.

We'd have strip steak and Palomas, talk of nothing much,

and dance.

Other novels featuring Ray Tatum are *Cry Me A River, Blue Ridge, Polar, Warwolf,* and *First In Flight.* These books were written to be read in no particular order.

An Amazon review would be much appreciated. Thanks for reading.

trp

Printed in Great Britain
by Amazon

83169486R00171